BEAUTY AND THE THORNS

STASIA BLACK

LEE SAVINO

Copyright © 2020 by Stasia Black and Lee Savino

All rights reserved. No part of this publication may be reproduced, distributed, or transmitted in any form or by any means, including photocopying, recording, or other electronic or mechanical methods, without the prior written permission of the publisher, except in the case of brief quotations embodied in critical reviews and certain other noncommercial uses permitted by copyright law.

This is a work of fiction. Similarities to real people, places, or events are entirely coincidental.

ISBN-13: 978-1-950097-44-9

Cover design by Jay Aheer

I never thought I'd see him again.
My first love, back from the grave.
My captor and tormentor.
He holds my past, present, and future in his scarred hands.
He owns me.
No matter how far I run, my path leads me back to that lonely castle.
Back into the arms of the Beast.

ONE

Present Day
Daphne

There's an engagement ring on my finger. How the hell did that just happen? I stare down in shock even as the click and flash of a hundred cameras go off, memorializing the moment. One second I was trying to think of how to do damage control and then Adam was down on one knee and then—

Logan. Oh gods. What did I just do? I'm going to be sick.

But Adam's grabbing my hand and holding it up, grinning at all the reporters. I never actually said *yes.* Not the words. I just sort of stared at Adam and gave a head bobble and then he shouted to the crowd that I *did* say yes and put the ring on my finger.

I do my best to keep the horror off my face. How could he do this? How could he put me on the spot like this?

Then I remember: Adam doesn't know. No one knows I've spent the last two weeks falling in l— I mean, becoming extremely close with another man. A man I've let master me. It's not hard to imagine Logan's fury when he finds out about this.

But that's not what's gutting me. It's knowing that underneath his anger and rage, I'll have hurt him. Hurt him so deeply.

Panic chokes me. No, I'll be able to explain it. I didn't have a choice. If I can just explain it, then he'll have to understand—

Adam pulls me close and mashes his mouth to mine. His tongue tries to invade my mouth but I seal my lips stubbornly shut. I can only be pushed so far. I understand I lose the company if I don't go along with this. I understand it might be the last shock that pushes my father's health over the edge if I don't agree with the farce.

But I can't betray Logan any more than I already have. I turn my face away from Adam and pull back, smiling at the crowd and waving.

"We have business inside now," I call out to the reporters. "Have to share the happy news!" And then I stride as quickly as humanly possible in these damn heels into the Belladonna offices.

TWO

Present Day
Daphne

"Oh Mama, it was awful," I cry, tears leaking down my cheeks. I sit, legs folded, beside her grave and the beautiful statue of her likeness, just like I used to do by her bedside.

Thornhill, my childhood home, looms in the distance like a comforting monument to sameness in the midst of all this change. This small ancestral graveyard is at the east edge of the property.

"I've made a mess of *everything*." I look up at her, beautiful and serene, the sunshine lighting the cold planes of her stone statue. It's nothing like her and yet better than anything else I have. Right now I'm clinging to anything of her I can get. I need her so much right now.

"Adam wanted to talk after the board meeting but I ran away like a coward after a few minutes. He's sincere and nice but he treats me like he's just going to come in and fix everything. Like I can't do anything myself. And gods, maybe I *can't*. Look at how I screwed it all up when I was CEO."

"And when I tried to tell him I couldn't marry him for real, he just said I was exhausted and that he'd take care of everything. Instead of fighting, I said he was right and I was going to go home and sleep. So then I was going to go straight back to Logan's to explain everything but instead I came here."

Thunder rumbles in the distance and clouds cover the sun, casting my mother's beautiful stone face in shadow. Like she, too, is turning her face away from me, wherever she is in the heavenly fields of paradise.

I bend over her grave, my tears falling and salting the ground. "Please," I beg. "Don't leave me alone. You always knew what to do. You knew how to handle Daddy when he was being impossible and you always made me feel better no matter how bad things got and I—"

"So *now* you show up at your mother's grave."

I choke out in shock at the voice and swing around. Logan! He's standing not five feet behind me. I jump to my feet and start to run towards him when I notice his face.

His features are cruel and angry.

He saw. He saw the news.

When he grabs my hand and holds it up, exposing Adam's ring still on my finger, I know for sure. He throws my hand away roughly in disgust.

"You lied to me," he spits.

"No, wait, Logan, it's not what you think—" I start but he swiftly cuts me off.

"Are you engaged to Adam fucking Archer?"

"I- I mean, well, technically, but not—"

Before I can get another word out, though, Logan's

crossed the few feet between us and his hand is at my throat. "Faithless whore," he spits. "Our bed wasn't even cold before you were off spreading your legs for him. I was just practice, I suppose, to break you in like a bitch in heat?"

I slap him. Hard. "You don't know what you're talking about."

His hand at my throat squeezes and he moves so that his face is only an inch from mine. And I can't help it. My body is trained to respond to his dominance. I liquefy beneath him. My curves soften to his hard muscle.

And he feels it. For a second, I see a glimmer of Logan, *my* Logan in his glittering blue eyes before they turn back to ice. "Is this how you were with *him*? Did your cunt soften and squirt when *he* touched you?"

He reaches down, roughly shoves up the skirt of my dress, and grabs my crotch. I have to fight my back arching into his touch.

"I ought to slap you again," I grit out through my teeth.

"Is that a yes?" he all but yells, gripping my sex harder as fury flashes in his eyes.

"No one but you has ever touched me there, *Master*!" I yell at him, just as furious. I know it looks bad, but doesn't he have any faith in me? In what we shared together? He wouldn't even let me tell him my side of things!

He just shakes his head at me. "I can't believe a word out of your lying mouth."

I deflate. So that's how it will be. The truth doesn't matter to him. Only his stupid, misguided vendetta. I shove him in the chest. "Then let me go," I shout, rallying again. "If you won't believe me, then there's no point in any of this."

He lets go of me and I stumble back.

"So that's it?" he laughs. "You and Adam Archer ride off into the sunset together? I don't think so, kitten."

I glare at him. "What do you *want* with me, Logan? You won't believe what I have to tell you."

"No." His dark eyes glare right back at me. "I won't ever believe anything that comes out of your lying mouth ever again. But that doesn't mean your debt to me is nearly begun being paid. I am your Master. And *I* get to say when you leave. Not you."

What? What does *that* mean?

"I- I don't understand," I say slowly.

"You will," he says darkly. "You will."

And then he rushes me, picks me up and slings me over his shoulder.

"Where are you taking me?" I squeal, banging on his back with my tiny fists and kicking uselessly. He locks his thick arm around my legs, holding them down, and walks towards Thornhill manor.

"I'm taking you home."

THREE

Present Day
Logan

She lied to me. She betrayed me. She's so warm and lithe and alive in my arms.

The fact that I still want her so badly burns worst of all.

I bang the front door to her childhood home open and let it slam into the wall.

"Logan, what are you doing?" she screeches. "Did you break in here?"

I smile maliciously as I kick the door shut. *Oh little kitten, I have so many surprises for you.* I swing her off my shoulder and down onto the expensive couch in the front sitting room.

"Why would I break into my own house?" I ask.

Her confusion is adorable. Truly adorable. I leave her in her muddle while I walk to the curtains and rip off the curtain tie, first one, then another.

She shrieks in protest. "What are you doing? My mother picked out those curtains!"

I nod. "Guess that's why nothing in this house has been updated in over a decade. I'll have to call in my interior decorator. She's a hot little thing who'll do anything for a buck. Probably even fuck me," I shrug.

"Why are you being so hateful? And what do you even mean, *your* interior decorator?" Daphne sits up and makes like she's going to stand but I'm on her before she can, pinning her down with my thigh.

I grab her wrists and wrap the curtain tie around them, binding them tightly. Her eyes flash up at me but she doesn't protest. She knows where this is going and she wants it as much as I do. I guess Adam couldn't satisfy her like I can. The thought both infuriates and gratifies me at the same time.

But mostly it just infuriates me. She's *mine*, but she gave herself to another man.

With a growl, I flip her over and I don't bother being gentle about it. Her ass sticking out in the air slightly mollifies me. I know there's only one thing that will truly soothe the beast inside me, though.

I hike her skirt up again. I plunge a finger inside her. She's wet and she doesn't protest. So the next second I yank my buckle open, shove my pants down, rip open a condom with my teeth and sheath myself. Then I shove my cock home.

"You bastard," she grunts, even as her perfect peach ass thrusts back up against me. Lying little— If I hadn't taken her virginity myself, I'd be questioning whether she'd just been playing virginal the whole time. But that tight cunt wasn't lying.

Even now, she's gripping me like a fucking vice. Not long ago she was a virgin and she's still tight as a drum.

But what if *he* was inside her, too? What if *he* tasted this sweet little cunt that's *mine*? If she shared herself because I never mattered more than a passing novelty, someone to get her off—

I fuck her more furiously but it's not the same. The condom is more than just a latex barrier between us. It's what it represents. I can't trust her anymore. What if she didn't use a condom with *him*? If my perfect, pure girl is now diseased because of that disgusting fuck?

My dick starts to lose its hardness and I yank out of her, breathing hard. Which only makes me more furious. How could she ruin everything like this?

I tear the condom off and throw it to the floor, then pull my pants back up. She looks over her shoulder at me but I grab her head and force her to face front again.

"Are you done?" she asks, more confused than mocking.

"Not nearly," I growl. I grab her and lift her, setting her on her feet at the side of the couch. "Bend over and grab the side."

She glares at me. "Go fuck yoursel—"

"Go ahead," I dare her darkly. "Finish that sentence."

She gulps and instead, lowers her head. Submitting. I breathe out, barely keeping my temper under control. "Grab the edge of the couch, ass out."

She stands still for a long moment, indecisive.

"You said you were only going to check on your father's well-being. Instead, you got engaged to another man. A man you know I hate. Don't you think you deserved to be punished for that?"

Her back goes ram-rod straight and I know she wants to say something. She wants to sputter her lies again, her fake 'explanations'. But she finally chooses to do the smartest thing she's done all day.

She bends over, wrists still bound.

I flip up her skirt.

"Logan, I—"

I bring my hand down before she can finish. And then I pull my belt out of the loops and snap the leather in the silence.

"It's time to begin your punishment. Count, kitten. Count and beg me for more."

FOUR

Present Day
Daphne

He's infuriating. Why am I going along with this? If he'd just *listen* to me!

Thwack.

"Ow!" I screech and look back at Logan furiously. He just spanked me. With his *belt*. And he has the gall to glare at me.

"Count. And then say, *may I please have another, Sir?*"

He's stoic. Furious. But not out of control. And underneath it, or maybe I'm imagining it, but underneath all of that, do I glimpse a glimmer of hurt?

What must it have been like, seeing me on TV like that? With Adam of all people, the man Logan considers his mortal enemy? Getting *engaged*?

Logan's not the sort of man to be able to listen until he

feels like he has a measure of control back. And this was how we've always been able to connect—this lightning shortcut to intimacy that made two weeks feel like a lifetime.

And I trust him. Even in his ice-cold anger. He might not trust *me* right now, but damn him, I trust him and I'm going to show him.

So, even though my ass is on fire, I don't drop his gaze as I say, "One. May I please have another, Sir?"

His arm moves back and he releases another *smack*.

Motherfu— My fingers dig into the fabric of the couch and I clench my stinging ass cheeks.

"Count," he demands ruthlessly.

"*Two*. May I please have another, Sir?"

The third follows before I'd barely gotten the words out. I dance in place at the pain. Ow! *Fuck*. How many of these does he have planned?

"Look how pretty your little ass is when it turns so pink. And it jiggles so good every time I smack it." He sounds mesmerized, then his voice turns dark. "Count for your Master. Count because I own you. Count because you're mine and I own this little pink ass. It's mine. *Count for me.*"

I nod and for some reason, I don't think it's the pain, tears start to course down my cheeks. He's hurt and I'm hurt. I *am* his but everything got all messed up and there's nothing I can do to fix it. Nothing except count and beg for this punishment.

"Four. M- May I p- please have another, Sir?"

There's a pause, and then another *thwack*, up higher this time, not in the same spot as before. My breath hitches and I blurt out, "Five. May I please have another, Sir?"

But then comes the touch of his large hand, hot but not

harsh. He probes my no doubt pink flesh. I start to turn my head to look over my shoulder but he orders, "Eyes forward."

I obey, dipping my head down to the arm of the couch, feeling more completely exposed than I ever have before in my life. Logan could destroy me if he wants. He always could.

But his touch...he's caressing me. Why is he caressing me?

"You're doing so well, kitten. Taking your punishment so well. Just five more. You're going to give me five more. Tell me you understand."

My lip trembles, but I nod and then manage a watery, "Yes, sir."

"Feel your Master's touch. Memorize it." His fingers move from the heated flesh of my ass cheeks down, down, down between my legs. In between. Skirting by my asshole, massaging as he goes. My breath hitches as he begins to tease at my sex.

He lingers, his fingers rubbing along my lips, whispering against my clit and making my sex clench and spasm around nothing, missing his cock. "Please," I whisper, not knowing what I'm asking for. More of his touch? His forgiveness?

But my words have the opposite effect. He snatches his hand away. "Count." His voice is ice cold again, and then comes the pain ripping across my ass as another blow lands.

"Six!" I screech. "May I have another, Sir?"

Another two land, one after another, never in the same spot twice, so I don't know where to brace to expect it. I dance on my toes at the burning heat that feels like it's searing through my flesh.

But that's when it hits me, clear as day: There's nothing

to do other than to give myself over to it. To stop fighting. To give myself to *him*, in spite of his anger.

Because this is Logan. *My* Logan. In spite of everything, I have to still believe, underneath, I haven't broken what we have—Daphne and Logan. He's not a beast, in spite of what I once thought. He's not using the full weight of his strength in these blows. He's being the Master, still caring for me even as he doles out punishment.

And to Logan, *my* Logan, I can trust and abandon myself over to whatever he has to give. My entire body relaxes as I give in.

When the next spank comes, it reverberates throughout my body. It still hurts. It hurts a hell of a lot. But I allow myself to feel the sting, the heat, and to ride it. To ride it all the way through my body and out again until a strange euphoria settles over me.

"Eight," I gasp. "May I please have another, Sir?"

Hesitation, and then the next comes. There's the pain, no less sharp for the euphoria, but while my feet are planted on the ground, I'm also floating. Floating so high. My breathing slows, my grip on the couch flexes and then releases.

"Nine, may I please have another, Sir," I manage in a rush, anticipating the last, all fear and confusion gone.

And when the last blow comes, it makes my body sing. For one shining moment, I feel so alive, my body electric, the world and all its worries a million miles away. I'm floating above it all. Safe like a cloud.

And then comes his touch. Hot where it already burns but then slipping between my legs and stoking another kind of fire. My face drops to the side of the couch. I'll go wherever he leads me. My body is pliant. I'm warm wax to be molded. "Thank you, Sir," I breathe.

"Damn you," he hisses. "Damn you."

His warm heat disappears from behind me. I blink in confusion, still spiraling down. When I look over my shoulder, all I see is him disappearing up the stairs.

What? Usually he never leaves my side after we— After a—

I swallow and stand up, wincing at the sting in my ass. My hands immediately go to my backside, but every touch hurts. I want to sit down. I feel woozy. I'm overwhelmed. I want to be in Logan's arms.

But he's not here. Why isn't he here?

Then there are footsteps on the stairs and my eyes fly up to see Logan coming back down, jar of salve in his hands. My entire body relaxes at the sight. He *is* going to take care of me. Tears spring to my eyes but I blink them back.

But then the jar of salve comes flying through the air at me and I lift my hands and catch it barely in time.

"I've called you a taxi." Logan's voice is low and arctic, his face blank of all emotion.

"I- I don't understand." And I don't. Everything still feels fuzzy after the places he just took my body. "This is my house."

Emotion lights his face now, but it's not one I like. A cruel smile curls his lips. "Your house. But *kitten*, your father sold me this property, too. All that was once yours is now mine. I own you."

His words snap me out of my daze. "Dad would never sell Thornhill! My mother is—!!" My eyes shoot to the window. I can't see my mother's resting place from here, but it's right out there. My *mom* is here, forever. All our memories are here. Dad wouldn't— He *couldn't*—

"Your father sold your ancestral home without a second thought to save his precious company," Logan continues.

"Without even consulting you. That's how much he values you and what you care about."

"And what are *you* going to do with it? Bulldoze the mausoleum and light my childhood home on fire to get your unholy revenge?"

"*Why shouldn't I?*" Logan rages, storming towards me, stopping only inches away from me, his face right in front of my face. The scars on his face are pale, but the rest of his skin is flushed and angry. "Your family took everything from me!"

I start to shake my head but he's not done, "And *you*," he growls. "Bella donna. Beautiful *poison*." He spits the last word and turns away.

His words gut me, scooping me out like an ice cream scooper.

For a long moment, there's only silence in the room, both of us breathing hard. We are destroyed things. Broken. Irreparable.

A sudden ping startles me. Logan pulls a phone out of his pocket. He doesn't look at me. "Your taxi is here."

My taxi. Just like that, he's kicking me out. Of my own house. That he bought out of revenge. This is so messed up.

I walk towards the door. What's there left to say?

"Don't forget the salve."

I look back at him searching for...something, *anything* in his eyes, but they're hard, blue stone.

I snatch the salve from where I'd dropped it on the couch before. And then I'm out the door. It's only after he slams it behind me and I'm in the taxi zooming away from my childhood home that I remember Belladonna. The company. The research.

Everything I worked my whole life for—he now has control of it. A man who hates me and my family.

I look out the window. It all seemed so important, so *vital*, only weeks ago. Like there was nothing more important in the world. But now, as I glance out the back window, my ass smarting even though the seat is soft and plush, all I'm hoping for is a glimpse of *him*.

FIVE

Present Day
Logan

I watch from an upstairs window as she drives away. Am I fooling myself or do I see her hand pressed against the glass of the window as she looks back?

I turn away. "Fucking *idiot*," I roar and look around for something else to smash but I've already tossed and smashed her precious Thornhill to ruins. Shards of expensive vases and mirrors and plates and glass litter the marble floors. I've ripped paintings off the wall and slashed through the precious canvases. I played Nine Inch Nails on full blast in the ballroom while I spray-painted the tapestries and drew obscenities on the statues.

The room I fucked and punished Daphne in was the one room that remained intact, and only because I fell asleep in the master suite last night before I could remember to drag my drunken ass back downstairs to desecrate it.

I stretch my hand out and bring it to my nose. It's still fragrant from her scent.

Her scent that *he* probably knows now. Because she gave away what's fucking *mine*. After she promised me, she gave it away. Like it all meant nothing.

I roar and grab the leg of the four-poster bed, ripping and yanking until I separate the tall pole off the footboard. And then I attack the wall with the makeshift baseball bat, smashing and destroying and taking out my rage until dust and drywall rains down all around me and coats my sweat-soaked skin.

I slump, exhausted, to the floor and bow my head. I didn't sleep last night. How could I? When I'm used to her warm body, when I let myself imagine getting used to it forever— The pain sears fresh all over again but I don't have the energy to destroy anything else. I lie down and lay my head on my arm. Cold. Uncomfortable. A shard of a vase cutting into my thigh.

And I sleep.

---

7 YEARS Ago
The Quarantine Ward

"I DON'T WANT to go in again. We flipped for it and you lost. You go."

Pain screams through my face as their voices wake me from another nightmare. But blinking my eyes open doesn't make it any better. Maybe this is the nightmare and I'm still not awake. Please gods, let this all just be one long nightmare and let me wake up.

But I don't wake. Because this is real. The pain, oh fuck, the pain. How did I even sleep as long as I did through this?

It's all real. Half my face is gone. Chewed away by flesh-eating bacteria. My life is gone. And she hasn't come to visit once in the month I've been here. Does she know what happened to me? Then again, why would they tell her? They were trying to get rid of me and they did a spectacular fucking job.

Quarantine plastic surrounds my hospital bed. I can just make out the shape of the two nurses beyond, and then one finally lifts a flap and slips through.

She's covered in a blue suit, face mask, and thick hospital gloves as she approaches cautiously. "Mr. Wulfe. How are we doing today?" Her falsely cheerful voice is grating.

I don't answer her asinine question. How the fuck does she think *we* are?

"Time to change your bandage."

That has me alert. "No," I manage to grunt out even though I immediately regret it because it pulls on my destroyed cheek and sends a fresh hell of blinding pain throughout my body.

That's the thing I didn't know about pain. The wound is just in my head but nerves are a strange thing. They seem to connect all over my body. And so the pain shoots everywhere. My face is on fire but I'll feel the pain in my belly. It curls me over into the fetal position.

"You know we have to change the bandage regularly to keep away infection," the nurse says, still in that fake cheerful tone.

They changed it last night and it's only ten in the

morning, I want to tell her, but I can't imagine getting out that many words. The final surgery to remove the last of the necrotic tissue and fluid was supposed to make things better but I swear the pain has only gotten worse. Maybe because they've dug away that much more of my face.

When I first came in, I coded twice in the ICU. It's been a month of this hell and a body can only stand so much.

But the nurse keeps coming relentlessly forward.

I try to shake my head but fuck, oh *fuck*, it hurts. I can't help the pathetic whimper that escapes or the tears that film my eyes. Dammit. Godsdammit.

The nurse reaches towards my face but I can see her fucking hands are shaking. She thinks she's gonna change my bandage with shaking hands? Fuck that.

I reach up to block her hands. She jumps back with a shriek at the barest contact. "Call the orderlies!"

She scurries back towards the plastic flap.

"Wait," I grate out, trembling from the pain of speaking. "Pain meds."

But she's already gone. The first few weeks, they gave me a morphine button but they said now I could only have pain meds at scheduled times to start weaning me off so I don't get addicted.

I flop my head back on the pillow, exhausted.

Daphne, where are you? It's a weak thought. I don't want her to see me like this. She's so young. And we never made each other any promises, not any real ones. We never even kissed. Why didn't I kiss her?

You were trying to be honorable. You were trying to respect her father.

I cough out a bitter laugh that has me curling over in pain.

"He's in here. He struck out at me. He's not in his right mind."

I blink up blearily at the voices. The nurse is back, but this time there are two orderlies with her. Big guys.

I don't get it at first, what they're all doing here.

"Be careful," the nurse warns. "He's the one with—you know. He's *the patient*."

The two big guys hold up their hands as they approach. That's when I see the fucking *restraints* they're holding.

"No." I start to sit up in bed, then immediately collapse back.

"We don't want any trouble. We just want to make it safe for everyone."

What did she tell them? That the monster in quarantine attacked her?

"I didn't—" I try to defend myself but speaking is so painful and it doesn't matter anyway. Their minds are already made up.

"Let me sedate him first," the second orderly says, like I'm not even in the room. He approaches with a needle.

The fuck? They think they can just knock me out and tie me the fuck up? For how long? I'm not a damned animal. I'm still a *man*.

But men can speak and reason and all I can do as they approach is grunt and shake my head and try feebly to hold them back. And finally thrash and scream until it takes both of them to hold me down to shove the needle in my arm until I descend into the nightmare hellscape of my dreams again.

"Logan!" calls out the beautiful girl with the green-flecked amber eyes. "Logan, where are you? I can't find you!" She's surrounded by fire and reaching out blindly.

I try to call for her but I have no voice and I can't move,

I'm tied down. I'm helpless as she's burned alive, and then the fire comes for me, burning, burning, the flame endlessly searing my body from the inside out.

PRESENT DAY

I JERK AWAKE, my hands immediately going to my face, then to my hands and wrists. Free. I'm not tied to that fucking hospital bed anymore.

Fuck, I haven't had the nightmares that take me back to that time in months. I scrub my face as I come back to myself, then get to my feet. I look at the destruction all around me and hear my mentor's voice in my head: Dr. Knox, who took me in when I was disfigured and broken, thrown away by everyone and anyone. *Don't expect life to be fair. This rage will do nothing but destroy you. Instead, use that energy to create. If you must destroy, destroy only those who are your enemies, not yourself.*

I was alone, cast away by everyone, locked away in that quarantine ward, when Dr. Knox found me. He made everything possible. He set me on my course. And for a while everything seemed so clear. *I* was clear. I had purpose and drive and I knew who I was.

But now?

"What do I fucking want?" I ask out loud, kicking out at a particularly large piece of vase that managed to survive, sending it flying across the floor and into the wall.

Her face immediately comes to mind.

Daphne.

I want her. I thought I wanted revenge but deep down, she's what I've always wanted.

Even if she doesn't want you back? Even if she's faithless?

I can never trust her, not now.

But I can still possess her.

Don't expect life to be fair. And possession is nine-tenths of the law. If she's mine, *he* can never have her. She'll be in my bed. Her ass under my belt, submitting so beautifully.

If I can't have love, then I'll break and enslave her to my mastery. No, she's not done with me. She'll never be rid of me. Not in this life or the next, I'll imprint myself so deeply on her. There will be no escape.

I stand and pull my phone from my trouser pocket. I pull up her contact and begin my message, then hit send:

OVER YOUR PREVIOUS STAY, YOU EARNED BACK 10 OF THE 130 BELLADONNA PATENTS I OWN. I'LL EXPECT YOU BACK AT THE CASTLE AT SUNDOWN TOMORROW TO BEGIN EARNING THE REST BACK.

Almost immediately, I see the icon that says she's read my text, but it's more than an hour before she finally texts back, just two letters, but they're all I need: OK.

SIX

Present Day
Daphne

"I don't understand." Rachel sounds as defeated as I feel.

I stay bent over my suitcase so I don't have to face her, but that just means I can't ignore the damn ring glittering on my finger.

"If I don't go back, we won't have a company. Belladonna will cease to exist."

"I can't believe all this," Rachel says. I told her the bare minimum, the castle, the patents. How I've been negotiating with Logan Wulfe, my father's former student, to take back ownership of my father's research.

I've left out the exact details of our negotiations. Especially how they involve me naked and bared to Logan's belt.

"You don't have to believe it. Just know I'll do what it takes to get those patents back. Whatever it takes." I force my cheeks to rise in a tight and tooth-achy smile. "It won't be like last time. I won't just disappear, I promise. I have my phone—" I hold up the cell with the freshly fixed screen. "And I'll check in."

"You better. Or I'll tell the press where you are."

My smile turns into a grimace. I can only imagine Logan's reaction to a flood of paparazzi on his lawn.

"I'll be fine, I promise."

Rachel's silence says it all. She doesn't believe me. Hell, I don't believe me. *But Logan would never really hurt me.* As angry as he was, he confined his punishment to a kinky game. *A kinky game we both love to play.* He wants a piece of ass, not a pound of flesh.

But he had wanted more. When he let me go, I saw the man he was, the couple we could be.

And then I threw it all away. Logan sees my actions as betrayal but I have to convince him otherwise. I have no choice. He holds my past, present and my future in his hands. *I own you.*

I unlock my phone and check my texts. The last one from Logan makes me shiver:

OVER YOUR PREVIOUS STAY, YOU EARNED BACK 10 OF THE 130 BELLADONNA PATENTS I OWN. I'LL EXPECT YOU BACK AT THE CASTLE AT SUNDOWN TOMORROW TO BEGIN EARNING THE REST BACK.

And my reply: OK.

ON MY WAY. I add. Then I tuck my phone in my pocket and close my suitcase. The zipper is loud in the quiet. The sound is so smooth and unwavering, so final.

"All packed," I say with mock cheer. "I called my dad and told him I'd be on break, but I'd check in." Dad was so excited—he'd already heard of my engagement from my goddamn fiancé. I kept the conversation short. "I put you down as a second emergency contact in case something happens and the nurse can't get a hold of me."

Rachel stirs. "What about Adam?" she asks.

My heartbeat stutters. I press a hand to my chest.

"Daphne? Are you okay?"

"Fine," I force out. I don't have time to be sick right now. I have to be okay. "I don't know what to do about Adam."

I finally face her. She's perfectly dressed and coiffed as usual, but she's wrapped one arm around her middle and the other crossed over her chest, protecting and comforting herself. Her face is wan and pale.

"I don't want to see him right now." Funny how I'm rushing back to Logan, the Beast who locked me up, but I can't stand the sight of the man who gave me a diamond ring.

My intuition is telling me something. I've numbed myself to it for years, but now it's waking from slumber.

Maybe that's why I'm so eager to head back to Logan. Somehow, somewhere in that castle I'll find my truth. It's been buried far too long.

Rachel holds my eyes for a long moment before she presses her lips together and nods. "Okay. Leave Adam to me. I'll hold him off."

"Thank you." I rush to hug her.

She squeezes me, then pulls back to look in my eyes. "Don't thank me. Just...take care of yourself, okay?"

I nod, not trusting myself to speak. Then, before I lose my nerve, I wheel my suitcase out the door. The cab is waiting to take me back to the castle.

Back into the arms of the Beast.

Because while he's the Beast, he's also...*Logan*. Sometimes the two barely fit together in my head and other times, I think, of course it was Logan all along. Of course only Logan could have ever made me feel so safe while I explored such wild things.

Only Logan would I have trusted to catch me when I leapt into the unknown. Only Logan could have known me better than I knew myself and how to draw me out.

Only Logan...*always Logan*.

SEVEN

8 Years Ago
Logan

I storm into the lab, that bastard Adam's voice ringing in my ears as he bragged about banging yet another college co-ed who was 'barely legal.' What a fucking bastard. I can't believe I ever considered that guy a friend.

When we both started working for Dr. Laurel, Adam showed me the same face he shows the rest of the world, polished golden boy, perfect in every way.

Until he realized I'm a nobody from nowhere. Then he didn't see the point and started shirking his work off onto me, not showing up, but still expecting to take equal credit for what's essentially become *my* work. Not that Dr. Laurel will hear a word against Adam, not the *perfect* Adam Archer. All he says is that we need to learn to get along if I want to keep my spot in the internship.

Fucking *infuriating*.

The door slams behind me and I hear a small yelp from the corner. I look up and freeze.

Because she's there.

Dr. Laurel's daughter. Soon to become a doctor herself, she's so close to getting her Ph.D. even though she's just a few months past eighteen.

She looks up at me, her eyes even larger and more luminous through her round bottle-glass lenses, which she immediately pulls off. But then she squints and puts them back on, running a hand through her hair and shyly saying, "Hi Logan."

"Oh. Hi." I cross the room over to the small study carrel at the edge of the lab where she has four huge textbooks open and a notebook with tiny scribbled notes covering the page.

As she looks up at me, her chest heaves up and down like breathing is suddenly becoming an issue for her.

And I'm immediately transported back to the ball a month ago. Walking up to her in that luminous toga that hugged all of her womanly curves, and watching the way she flushed so prettily when I spoke to her.

Not that it stopped her from gathering the courage to ask me to dance.

I don't dance. Not even for you, I told her.

I meant to say more, to invite her to go for a walk, maybe out to one of the balconies where we could hear ourselves think beyond the unnerving roaring chatter of the ballroom.

But no.

Adam fucking Archer swept in and grabbed her, smirking at me as he led her onto the dance floor in my place.

He doesn't care about Daphne. He barely speaks to her.

But she was beautiful, the center of attention, and he could tell in that moment I wanted her.

But he's not here right now. It's just me and her.

And unlike him, even in her oversized sweater, tortoise shell glasses and her hair in a haphazard bun, I can see that she's just as beautiful now as she was the night of the ball.

Her face has thinned out as she's transformed from girl to woman while the rest of her body has softened. The tight leggings she's wearing show off her curves as she curls up in her chair, one knee to her chest.

"What are you studying?"

"Ugh." She makes a face. "Stem cell research applied to Myelodysplastic syndrome. I mean, it's really fascinating. And it could have implications towards Dad's research trying to help Mom. They harvested stem cells from my cord blood when I was born, knowing it might help Mom—"

I close the books and her notebook. "When was the last time you ate?"

It seems to me her whole life, her Dad has considered his wife's needs before his daughter's. Maybe it's not my place. I don't know what I would do if my spouse was sick, but he barely spends any time with Daphne, when she kills herself to please him studying, getting early degrees so she can join him in the lab, and spending all her free time nursing her sick mom.

She looks distracted, her eyes going back to her books guiltily like she feels like she ought to be studying—as if even the thought of taking a break seems selfish.

Which makes me grab the back of her chair and pull it out from the carrel. "No more excuses. We're going out for a bite."

Her bright green eyes flash up at me. "We are?"

I give a firm nod. "We are."

A small smile lights her face. "Okay."

Good girl, I think but don't say. The thought immediately discomfits me, though. Especially when her instant obedience has my jeans tightening. I stand back and frown as she grabs her jacket. Shit, I can't be thinking that way about her. And not just because she's the boss's daughter.

Admiring her beauty is one thing, but she's still way too young. Too naïve for the shit I'm into, especially lately.

You don't tie nice girls like her up and spank them.

My balls tighten at the image that flashes through my head but I'm not a jackass, so I force it away.

She barely has any friends. That's all I'm being.

She grabs her purse and then we're walking together towards the elevator. The silence feels heavy as we ride up to the first floor. She glances my way and her cheeks turn rosy. What's she thinking about? Is she hoping I'll grab hold of her and kiss her like they're always doing on those soapy doctor dramas on TV?

The thought makes me smirk and she immediately looks away, her cheeks going even pinker. So, so innocent. Which makes something in my chest hurt because it's a rarity.

The ping of the elevator arriving at the first floor startles both of us. She laughs self-consciously and then hurries off.

We settle in at a sandwich shop across the street from the lab. "How's your mom doing?" I ask after we've ordered and sat down.

"She's doing okay." Daphne nods enthusiastically. "I'm really hopeful about the new rounds of treatment you, Dad, and Adam have been working on. I spent the morning with her and she was sitting up and we did the crossword. Well, we managed half of it before she got too tired, but I feel like it's progress." She bites her lip but keeps nodding, like she's trying to convince herself more than me.

I can't help reaching across the table and taking her hand. "Daph, it's me. You don't have to bullshit with me. I know everyone else asking you always wants to hear that she's doing better, but I know her condition. You don't have to put a pretty spin on shit for me."

She looks a little surprised, maybe because I cursed in front of her, but then she nods, and finally she doesn't look like a bobblehead. "Yeah," she breathes out, her chest deflating a little. "It's still really hard, actually. I mean, this morning was better than most, but it's still..."

She looks out the window and tears film over her eyes. She immediately blinks them away, then drops her head like she was embarrassed for me to see.

Fuck, who taught her she had to be like this? I can't stand to watch it so I scoot my chair around the table and nudge her chin up with my hand. "Hey, Champ, you know it's okay to be sad, right?"

She glares at me and jerks back. "I'm not a child."

"Oh believe me, I know," I mutter darkly.

Her breath hitches. "What does that mean?"

The waitress comes by and delivers our food. "Nothing. Eat your sandwich."

Daphne's still frowning at me, but again, does as she's told. She only takes a tiny, nibbling bite, though.

"Woman, you aren't a bird. Take a full bite."

She finishes chewing and lifts an eyebrow at me. "So you've noticed I'm a woman now?"

"I don't know, Champ, you've only been one for what?" I look at my wrist and a nonexistent watch, "About three minutes?"

She throws her napkin at me. "Try three months."

I shrug. "Pot-*a*-to, pot-*ah*-to."

She mock glares at me but does take larger bites of her

sandwich, though she only finishes half of it before abandoning it on her plate. In the same amount of time, I've devoured my entire sandwich and bag of chips, along with most of my soda. I learned early not to waste food when it was put in front of me.

When I look up from inhaling my food, I find Daphne observing me, her brow slightly scrunched. I swipe at my mouth with a napkin.

"What?" Shit, she's probably used to more manners. Adam fucking Archer probably eats sandwiches with a silver-plated knife and fork.

"Nothing, I just wonder about you sometimes. Where do you come from? What's your life like when you aren't at the lab? You're kind of a mystery, Logan Wulfe."

I choke a little on my sip of soda. The thought of innocent Daphne knowing about my activities outside of the lab is enough to almost have me doing a spit-take.

I haven't been with a woman for a few months...not since I saw Daphne at the ball now that I think about it, but still. Just because I haven't had time for it doesn't mean my proclivities aren't a very real part of who I am.

I just shrug but she's not about to let it go. "For real, Logan. I want to know more about you. Like, where did you grow up? You never talk about your family."

I shrug again. "It's cause I don't have any. Dad was a deadbeat. Walked out on my mom when I was too young to remember. We were poor as f— We were poor. My mom tried for as long as she could but..."

I look up into Daphne's compassionate amber eyes. "She wasn't like you. She never had your kind of strength. The world was too much for her. She could barely take care of herself, much less me. So I mostly raised myself till she decided to check out."

I can tell by the confusion in her eyes she's not translating my euphemism. "She committed suicide."

Daphne's hand shoots across the table and grabs mine. "How old were you?" she whispers.

I shrug but don't pull my hand away from hers. I don't know why. I'd pull away from anybody else. Maybe, I don't know, maybe it's because Daphne didn't have much of a childhood either. Her parents were just selfish in different ways, her dad at least, and her mom too sick to take care of her. As far as I can see, she raised herself as much as I did—she just did a fucking better job of it than me.

"I was twelve."

"*Logan.*"

"Look, it's no big deal." I try to pull my hand away now but she just clenches tighter.

"Somebody wise once told me it's okay to be sad."

"Oh yeah? Sounds like a real wise ass."

"He has his moments." She smiles at me and it's so genuine and from her heart it hits me straight in my gut.

Where have you been my whole life? What I say out loud is, though, "Wanna go grab dessert from that little pastry place on 4th street?"

She beams at me. "I'd love to."

When we stand up, she's still holding my hand.

EIGHT

Present Day
Logan

The cameras pick up the approach of Daphne's taxi two hundred feet from the gates of the castle. I press the button to open them and sit with my fingers loosely threaded together as the car creeps up the long drive. My heart jolts when I catch a glimpse of Daphne's dark head. I hate myself for missing her, but I did. This girl has always been under my skin, in my blood.

I spin in my chair away from the cameras, rising and stretching with eyes closed. *Calm. Control.*

This time it'll be different. I have her stay planned down to the hour. Her tasks and trials, the way she'll serve me. My own version of the twelve labors of Hercules, tailored to train her to my whims.

I just can't let myself feel. The softness of her skin, her honeyed scent, the golden glint in her green eyes—

nothing will move me. I am the Master. She is mine. Even when others in her life tried to steal her, she returns to me.

I turn back to the cameras. The cab is gone, leaving Daphne and her sole suitcase. Her hair blows in the wind. She makes her way to the door, her hips swaying with unconscious grace.

My heart, the stupid, weak organ, stutters. *She's returned to me.*

Maybe it can be different, I think as she stands on the stoop, reaching for the iron knocker with trepidation in her eyes. Maybe we can start over.

Then she pulls out her phone, stepping away from the stone wall to get service. The fucking engagement ring glitters on her finger as she raises the cell to her ear.

What the fuck? She's still wearing Adam's mark. Is she calling *him*?

Déjà vu. A scarlet curtain falls. The mindless rage rising.

I find myself at the front door, a hand on the latch.

No! Calm. Control.

This time it *will* be different. I'll stay in control. And I won't let myself feel.

I'll be the soulless monster she believes me to be.

Daphne

"WAIT, WHA—!" But Logan doesn't wait or explain as he hoists me up over his massive shoulder, his arm a bar across the back of my legs, locking me in place. "Logan!"

I've only just barely gotten in the door of his castle and this is what he pulls.

"Don't call me that," he growls. "Call me Beast or Master because that's all I am to you now."

"Son of a bit—"

I yelp at the sharp smack that earns me across my ass that's still sore from our last session. "No more spanking. I can't handle any more. I've barely been able to sit down. Please."

"Please, what?" he demands as he walks down the stairwell to the basement, not winded or off balance by my weight in the slightest bit.

I grind my teeth together but my ass really is too sore for any more abuse. "Please, *Master*." Alright, so that *Master* might have been dripping with sarcasm. And he doesn't miss that because it earns me another sharp smack on the ass.

I screech but then hurriedly squeak out, "Yes, Master!"

"That's better." I can hear the smile in his voice, the smug bastard.

I'm so off-kilter, I can barely take in my surroundings. But I still recognize it when he takes me straight to the dungeon. Because of course he does. My entire stay is probably going to be in this damn place. The stone walls, the familiar musty smell that I've missed even though I've been away from it for such a short time... Why am I excited instead of scared?

Because Logan is Master, a voice whispers from deep within.

I glance around at the cross set up against the wall, all sorts of implements hanging here and there. A bench I think is meant for...for spanking. And a table that he walks straight over to and deposits me on.

"Take off your clothes."

I bite my lip and hazard a glance at Logan. His face is cold, devoid of emotion. I glare at him and do as he says. I pull off my shirt and bra quickly and efficiently. It's not a strip tease. I kick off my jeans and leave them in a pile at my feet. The same with my underwear.

I'm not quite sure how I manage to stand, back straight, completely naked in front of him, but I do. He doesn't look down at my body. Doesn't even peek.

"Get on the table."

In for a penny, in for a pound. My heart starts racing a hundred miles an hour but I hop up on the table and lay down.

There are cuffs at the wrist and ankles that Logan begins to swiftly attach to me, tying me down.

And...and...I- I-

I'm thrilled.

I lay my head back and close my eyes as I silently admit to myself what I'll never ever say out loud. I'm back where I belong. My toes flex in anticipation. I have absolutely no idea what Logan, what my *Master*, will do to me.

But I trust him. This is the boy who noticed I was lonely and took me for sandwiches all those years ago. And the man who demands things of my body I never knew I had to give. I've never felt more alive or in my body than right this second.

"Look at you," Logan croons, the first time his voice has softened even the slightest bit since I've arrived. "Your body is quivering for my touch. You want this, don't you?" He skims his fingers up my thigh. "You want this bad."

I can't help quivering in response and I try to stop my gasp but don't manage in time.

"Well, today, little girl, is going to be your first trial. And your first lesson. You can't always get what you want."

I frown. What does *that* mean?

Logan prowls around the table.

"Did you learn about the twelve labors of Hercules in school?"

I nod. "I think so. It sounds familiar. But I- I don't remember the particulars."

"Hercules too committed a great sin, and so in penance, the oracle told him to go serve King Eurystheus and do all that he asked of him. The King set him to twelve labors, each more difficult than the last."

Logan bends over me, eyes blazing into mine. "The last task had him descend into the very bowels of hell itself." He trails a finger gently down my face and then between my breasts, pain and anger etched between his brows. "Are you willing to go to hell and back for your sins, Daphne?"

I strain against my bindings. *I didn't commit the sins he's bound and determined to think I did,* I want to scream. Why is he so determined to think the worst of me? What's happened to him to make him like this? The boy I once knew and even the man of the last two weeks I've become so intimate with... Finding Logan again only to lose him—I can't. I *won't*.

So I tell him the truth. "I'm willing to do it for *you*." I'll fight for him, dammit. For this. For *us*.

For a second, just for the briefest flicker of a moment, I think I see something in him crack—a flash of the Logan I know and cherish.

But the next second the Master is back, cold and calculating. He pulls back and stands up straight, turning away from me.

"Then let us begin."

NINE

7 Years Ago
Daphne

"How did I know I'd find you here?"

I look up at hearing my favorite voice, butterflies alight in my stomach.

Logan.

He pays attention to me out of pity, I know that's why. But still my heart soars every time he stops by to say hi, and the few times he's taken me out to eat—*heaven.*

"Hi Logan." I try for my voice not to sound shy but don't quite succeed. *Gods, don't look like a timid little girl!* I thought there was maybe a moment at the Ubeli's ball when he saw me as more...but then he wouldn't dance with me and I barely saw him the rest of the night.

"How long have you been hunched over your books here?" he asks. "I saw you when you came in this morning and that was hours ago. Have you been at it all night?"

I blink blearily and glance over at the clock on the wall, then down at my laptop. "I was trying to finish this chapter on my dissertation and I guess time got away from me."

His brow furrows. "Have you had any sustenance other than coffee?" He gestures at the several empty coffee cups in the corners of my little study carrel.

A thrill goes through me in spite of my tiredness. Does this mean he's about to take me on one of our little lunch dates? Then I wince internally. No, they aren't *dates*. I'm a pity project and he's a good man afraid of a girl on his watch dying of starvation.

He lifts an eyebrow. "Woman cannot live on coffee alone. Come on."

Woman. He called me *woman*.

He was making a joke. Don't be an idiot.

But I'm nodding and getting to my feet. "Okay, if you say so." Inside, I'm doing cartwheels. Logan date! Logan date!

I'm too tired to fight the internal battle and allow myself to just be happy as he leads me to our favorite sandwich shop.

But to my surprise, he gets our order to go.

My heart sinks. No Logan date after all. He's just seeing that I'm fed and taking me right back where he found me. Dear heavens, this is embarrassing.

I stand up straighter and try to be a grown-up about the whole thing. "Look, Logan. I appreciate it but really, I can take care of myself. Let me just pay for this, then I'll get out of your hair."

I try to reach for my wallet in my purse but he puts his big, warm hands on mine, stopping me.

Logan Wulfe is touching me. I melt under the contact,

especially when I look up and those intense blue eyes are locked on mine.

"Daphne, it's okay to let someone look out for you once in a while. And after all your father has done for me, it's the least I can do to provide his hungry daughter a meal once in a while. Please?"

It's not so much that I agree as I'm stunned into silence by the earnestness of his blue eyes and his touch, so he gets his way.

My hand feels terribly cold as soon as he lets me go to reach for his own wallet to pay the clerk.

At least I know why he looks out for me now—it's not pity, or maybe it is, but it's also obligation and gratefulness to my father. It still has nothing to do with me.

But, sad sap that I am, I'll still cling to every moment I have with Logan.

I expect him to take us right back to the lab but instead, our lunch in one hand, he *takes my hand* with his other and leads us down the sidewalk away from the lab.

Holy crap, holy crap, holy crap, Logan Wulfe is holding my hand!!!

What does it mean? Does he—? Oh crap, is my hand sweaty? If I would've known he was going to pull this move, I would've wiped it on my jeans first.

He lets my hand go almost as quickly as he grabbed it, though, leaving my head a tornado of swirling thoughts.

But he's grinning at me, that strong jaw and brow so masculine, it kills me. While Adam Archer is what most people would describe as classically handsome, Logan is what does it for me. Rough around the edges, but a sweetness that belies his difficult youth.

And he's *real* in a way that Adam isn't. Adam is like the fake sweetener that's so overly sweet, it makes everyone like the drink, but only because they can barely taste the original substance anymore.

Whereas Logan is black coffee. Bracing. Honest. Of the earth. And so, so good.

"We're going for a day-trip."

"What?" I almost cough the word, I'm so surprised. But then I realize Logan's stopped us in front of a truck.

"Being stuck in that lab all the time isn't good for you. You need some vitamin D." He unlocks the passenger side door and opens it for me, gesturing me inside.

Squee, Logan date back on!

I don't hesitate scrambling up inside, especially when he holds out a hand to help me.

When he rounds the truck and climbs in, I'm all but bouncing on the seat in my excitement. "Where are we going?"

He smirks, glancing at me. "It's a surprise. But it's a ways away. Do you want to eat now or when we get there?"

"When we get there." I love watching Logan eat and I'm used to going without food.

"Okay, then you should get some rest."

It's a warm day, but he still pulls out a light blanket from the back seat and arranges it over me. It's seriously the sweetest gesture and stupidly, I tear up.

I turn my face towards the window. People don't do this sort of stuff for me. I'm the one who takes care of Mom, and Dad, too. He's like me, forgetting to eat, going days without sleep. I get lost in the shuffle and it's okay, I completely understand. He's trying to save Mom's *life*.

But...Logan looking out for me, regardless of why he's doing it— He'll never know how much it means to me.

So I curl up in the blanket and, regardless of how

excited I am to spend every second possible with him, I do as he asks. I fall asleep.

When I wake up, I can't help my yelp of delight.

"Oh, Logan!" I sit up straight, the blanket falling to my lap.

The beach. He's taken me to the beach. It's only three hours away, but I've only been once before in my whole life. But then again, this is Logan Wulfe, the man of my dreams, who makes dreams come true.

TEN

Present Day
Logan

Daphne's tied down and spread out on the table like a sacrifice on an altar. Her body is a gift to the gods, lithe and tight with the perfect amount of curves.

Tonight I'm her god.

She obeyed me so quickly, maybe I should go easy on her for this first trial. Her pussy pouts at me, soft and slick with wanting.

Or maybe she obeyed because she craves this.

I lay a hand on her flat belly and she whimpers. I chuckle, "You need this."

Her hips rise. "Logan, please."

I drop my hand and step away, clenching my hands to fists. How easily she pulls me back in. I can't forget what this is. Well, I'll prove it to both of us. Right here and right now. "I told you not to call me that."

"Master," she pants.

"Better. But too late." I return with the wooden box that holds her nipple clamps. Her cries won't move me, and certainly not my name on her lips. I'm here for one thing and one thing only. To master her. She is mine to train. *Mine*.

"One day I'll pierce you," I murmur as I lever the clamps onto her poor nipples. Her breath hisses through her teeth, but she doesn't beg me to remove them. "Would you like that?"

"Whatever my Master wishes," her voice is low and throaty. Her eyes are large and dark with pupils blown. Into subspace so soon?

"You say that now." I head down to the end of the table where I can lean between her legs. "I wonder if you'll regret it when you discover what I have planned for you." I spread her labia, inspecting her almost clinically. Her breathing ramps up and her juices pour. My fingers come away sticky. I raise my hand to my face and drink in her scent. Mouth-watering.

"I wonder..." My finger is huge compared to her delicate parts. I use my index finger to nudge the sensitive spot next to her clitoris. How large can it get? I'm her Master and she's my sub. My job is to take her to her limits so that's what I'll do.

She twists her body, letting out a long, keening moan.

I slap her thigh lightly. "Quiet! This isn't for your pleasure."

Her cry shudders from her, her pussy growing even more wet. As if my command aroused her. She's so responsive, so attuned to my touch.

"I just want to see...yes..." Her clitoris is swollen stiff, peeking from its hood. "There you are." I tickle alongside the hardened nub, driving her towards orgasm. Her panting increases, but at the last second, I stop.

"Noooo," Daphne moans. My own cock stiffens.

"Silence," I order. *Oh beautiful Daphne, how much you have to learn.* "If I want you to beg, I will ask for it." I'll gag her if necessary. She would look so beautiful, bound and gagged, green eyes begging me for relief.

Even now her chest is flushed and heaving. The jeweled clamps twinkle with every rising and falling breath.

I hold up the third clamp and wait for her to realize my plan. Her eyes grow huge.

"Oh yes," I let a wicked grin claim my lips. I can't help it. A Master can stay in control and enjoy himself too, right? "As promised."

She trembles slightly as I approach with the clit clamp in hand. The one I've chosen is the most benign, a beginner's clamp. A bit of lube and the teardrop head will easily fit over her clitoris, with the long wire legs clamping her labia. Several jewels hang from either end.

"You'll look so pretty for me. Maybe I'll clamp you and make you serve me dinner." A meal with her naked and panting. Whenever she bent to place food in front of me, I'd tweak the clamps tighter…

As I fit the clamp into place, Daphne cranes her head to watch. She doesn't seem too horrified. No, she looks fascinated.

"My curious little deviant."

This is her power, isn't it? Everywhere I lead her, she so enthusiastically follows. No hesitation. Her hips roll and the muscles of her stomach ripple. Her eyes grow hooded, her lashes fanning over her flushing cheeks.

I'm attuned to every twitch, every hitched breath, every eyelid flutter. I am her Master, her maker.

Her god.

The clamp fits perfectly, squeezing her delicate flesh. The jewels hang down, tickling her perineum. The emeralds glisten with her juices.

I bend down, intent as a scientist looking through a microscope. Watching miracles unfold. I toy with the jewels and she clenches her bottom. I blow on her clit and she rocks her hips. All the while, desperate little gasps escape her lips.

"Poor Daphne." I rise a moment, adjusting myself. My cock is stiff and throbbing in my pants. I'm torturing myself as much as torturing her.

I roll up my shirt sleeves and settle in for my feast.

At the first touch of my tongue, her back arches, her body bowing as far as she can go in the restraints. "Master," she screams.

My cock almost splits my pant's seam. I nuzzle the clamp with my nose and glide my tongue over her quivering flesh.

We groan in unison. Her sweet taste— "Heaven."

Daphne

I KNEW Logan would torture me when I returned, but I might not survive a day. Logan's face is pressed between my legs, freaking eating me like he's starving.

My wrists are red from tugging at my bounds. I'm desperate to grab his face and grind down. I'm so close—

Logan pulls away, wiping his face on his shirt sleeve. Leaving me on the edge. *Fuck!*

"You can't always get what you want," Logan intones. Fucker.

My arousal teeters on a knife edge. One side pleasure, the other side pain. Or maybe the two are one.

But I feel a rush of gratitude. If this is all my Master will dish out, then I can take it.

"You took your clamping well."

I relax at the praise. The jeweled clamp didn't look too scary. Just a wire prong designed to squeeze my flesh a little bit. Maybe I'll survive tonight after all.

He adds a touch of lube and slides the prong off. The way he's watching my face, I know something's about to happen. And then, it does. Holy shit!

The blood rushes back to those places.

Oh fuck, oh fuck!

My clit is engorged a thousand-fold. I stare down between my legs but can barely concentrate because I'm about to explode, right on the edge. It's so close, so insane, I've never felt such a buildup of pleasured intensity—

I writhe my hips this way and that, trying to get stimulation. Maybe I can catch my clit on the side of my leg—

"Ah ah," Logan steadies me, adding restraints that pull my legs further apart. He leaves for a moment, exiting into the shadows.

I lay on the table, half-floating, my throbbing clit my only tether to the earthly plane, a red beacon in the blissful haze. What is it about this man that makes me just…surrender?

The Beast returns. He is the Beast now, fully. A mask affixed to his features. A hulk of a man, my body recognizes as Master. My toes curl at the sight of him—shirt off, muscles on display. In his hand: a black crop.

Maybe the pain's just begun. My heart trips over itself

as he runs the black leather flap along my face and neck, tracing my collarbone, circling my breasts.

Whap! The crop strikes the underside of my right breast. A cruel sting on my soft flesh. Why is my pussy flooding?

Whap! Another on the inside of my thigh. A bright patch on the smooth pale skin. Why does my back arch, offering my body up?

More soft strikes and sudden strikes. The crop rubs my pussy folds and comes away coated in moisture. Master holds it to my lips to taste. Tart and salty. Why does it taste so good?

My body is covered with red marks. Brilliant ornaments. My Master is a genius, to paint my flesh so well. He took a blank canvas and made it beautiful. I am his masterpiece.

"You've been so good." Master's crop nudges my pussy folds, sparking new pleasure. His voice comes from far away. "But Daphne? We're just getting started."

He brings the crop down on my pussy. *Thwap!* Fireworks burst behind my eyes. A scream rings in my ears. My throat is raw—the sound was torn from me.

Master strokes the leather lovingly down my legs. "I bet I could make you cum just from this. But no. You don't deserve to cum."

Tears slide from my eyes, glazing a path to my temples. I want to deserve what Master gives me.

The Beast leaves. The Beast returns. He has another gift for me in his hands. A wicked looking tweezer clamp with silicone-tipped ends. He aligns it with the seething bundle of want that is my clit. Squeezes down.

"Oh, fuck!" I lose control of my tongue.

"Naughty girl." He crops my breast again, making the

jewels bounce. *Yes!* Punish me. Make me pay. I'll take the pain. I'll deserve the good things I want.

This is where I'm meant to be.

LOGAN

HER TEARS DON'T MOVE me at all. Nor her breasts, reddened from the crop strikes, wearing the emeralds so proudly. Her supple thighs, shimmering with sweat and her cunt juices. Her godsdamned scent...

I turn my back on her, turn away to adjust myself. My arousal makes me grit my teeth. I wish I could explain away my erection. *I haven't cum in a while. Wielding a crop always makes me hard.* But it's Daphne. All Daphne.

She betrayed you. Lied to you.

But she's so beautiful, her tears so earnest, her face and body so...so fucking *necessary*. I don't want to want her, but I do. I always have.

"You will learn," I growl and grit my teeth. The crop falls over and over, leaving red in its wake. She cries out, the slim column of her throat working as she labors to draw breath. She's close to the boundaries of where I wanted to take her. Any further and there'll be danger. Too much damage. Too much pain.

Calm. Control. I am the Master.

Who am I fooling? When it comes to Daphne, I am undone.

The crop slices down, striking her between her legs. The clamp goes flying.

Her body stiffens and a wail breaks from her, long and

unending. I drop the crop and stare at her heaving body. Her eyes open wide, unseeing, her fingers clenching and unclenching as her orgasm goes on and on.

She just came from excruciating pain.

She's one in a billion. But then, she always was.

ELEVEN

7 Years Ago
Daphne

"You drove for three hours? To take me to the beach?" I'm still incredulous.

Logan just shrugs. "So let's enjoy it."

Now I'm speechless. But he's already out of the truck, popping his seat and pulling things out of the small compartment behind it. Beach towels. A full backpack. Our lunch.

I only realize that I'm still sitting there, stunned, when he glances my way and smirks. "You just gonna sit there or you coming?"

I shove my door open and hop out of the car.

By the time I come around to him, he's pulling things out of the backpack.

"Here, there's some bathrooms over there where you can go change." He hands me a bag.

I grab it and look inside. Holy crap, he bought me a bathing suit. I pull it out excitedly...until I realize it's a one-piece, and not just a one-piece, but one that looks like it was designed a hundred years ago. It even has a little skirt at the bottom. Does he think I'm five?

I glance over to where he said I could change. It's a sunny day in mid-summer and the beach is buzzing with people. And right beside the restrooms is a little shop.

I smile breezily up at Logan. "I'll be right back."

"I'll go find us a place on the beach," he says.

"Perfect."

He walks me to the bathrooms, then continues on to the beach. I wait until he's out of sight, then duck inside the small shop.

They don't have a huge selection of bikinis, but I find one that will do. It's bright red and while it covers the important bits, it also shows *plenty* of skin. After I buy it along with some flip-flops, I change in the bathroom. But I only dare a few seconds of looking at myself in the mirror.

I've never worn anything so skimpy in my entire life. And I'm going to go spend the day with Logan in this thing?

Maybe I should abandon ship and just put on the swimsuit he brought for me.

But then I hold up the shapeless, dark, unflattering thing, and with one last glance in the mirror at all my curves on display in the red bikini, toss the other swimsuit in the trash and head out the door.

Confident. Wear the swimsuit, don't let the swimsuit wear you.

The only way Logan will ever start to see me as a woman is if I act like one. But crap, how do women act? I don't know any women other than Mom, and she's so sick...

I blink away the thought. Gods, it's horrible, but for one

day I want to just be a girl at the beach with a cute guy. It's a terrible thought to have. *I'm* a terrible person for having it.

By then I've walked down the little path and I see Logan in the distance. He's standing with his hand over his eyes looking my way. He doesn't realize it's me until I get really close, though. Understandably, since he's looking for a dowdy girl in that terrible swimsuit.

When I wave and he finally realizes that I'm the one walking up to him, red bikini and all, he does a double take. And then he swallows really hard.

"What are you wearing?" he demands in a voice harsher than I've ever heard from him.

It makes me bite my lip for a second, but then I straighten my spine.

"I'm supposed to get Vitamin D, right? I can't do that if I'm all covered up. I picked this up at the little shop."

He looks away towards the ocean, his jaw tensing so hard, I can see a vein on his neck popping out. He gives a single sharp nod.

Things are tense for a few moments as I settle myself on the towel beside him. He sits at the furthest edge of the towel from me, half on the sand. And he won't look at me.

But that's okay, because it gives me the opportunity to look at *him*.

I didn't realize it earlier, but the shorts he was wearing were swim trunks, so all he had to do was take off his shirt.

And holy *moly*.

He's not huge or anything. He actually looks younger without his shirt on. I bet when he's older he'll be big—his shoulders are already really wide but they haven't quite filled in all the way.

But he's still so much bigger than me. And there's this crazy sexy dusting of hair across his pecs.

Sexy.

That is the word for Logan Wulfe. He. Is. So. Sexy.

He's leaning back casually on his elbows, the salty wind blowing in his hair, his tan skin shining in the sun.

My stomach swoops with feelings I've never felt before. All I know is that I want to crawl on top of him. I want to bury my face against his chest and have him wrap those arms around me.

The swoopy, liquid feeling in my tummy zings lower, between my legs and I inhale sharply, which makes Logan look my way.

Our eyes catch. Oh crap, oh crap, can he tell what I'm thinking? Does he know I've just been ogling him for the past five minutes and that I'm having sexy feelings about him?

Is it just me feeling like there's a sizzling intensity in his eyes as we continue to lock gazes? Am I imagining his nostrils flaring? His eyes darkening? Could he possibly feel even a morsel of what I'm feeling back?

"Want to go for a swim?" he finally says, his words an explosion of air as he hops up from the blanket. "I'm going for a swim."

He's already walking away from me before I can agree and jump up to join him.

But he slows down as I hurry after him and he holds out a hand to me as I unsteadily follow him into the water.

"You've swam in the ocean before, right?" he checks.

"Once. A long time ago. I was a kid though and it was mainly splashing on the shore."

He mutters something under his breath, I think about my dad, but then he moves closer. "Stay beside me."

I nod as we move into the water up to our hips and the incoming waves are stronger.

"Okay, now let's start to swim. Once we get past that break it should settle out."

I nod as he lets go, following him and abandoning my feet on the ground as we start to swim along the shoreline.

The ocean swells with a small wave, but we swim through it and avoid the whitewater of the break.

"You're doing great," he encourages.

The truth is I'd be terrified if I was out here by myself. But with him, I feel invincible.

We don't go far and he warns me about undercurrents. We hang out and I'm exhilarated by riding the swells of the waves.

"Oh my gosh, here comes a big one. Logan, look how big it is!"

"I've got you," he laughs, swimming over to my side. "We'll ride it together."

I nod as he holds onto me from behind, his arms wrapped around my waist. I hold out my arms and tread water as the biggest swell yet comes.

"Swim towards it," Logan says in my ear.

I do, and I feel like I'm flying with him so close. The swell comes and we rise so high, so high, it feels like breathing with the huge animal that is the ocean. And then down we come as the wave crashes down.

I laugh and spin in Logan's arms.

I want to kiss him but I wouldn't even begin to know how. So I hug him instead. "Thank you. Thank you, Logan. You don't know how much this means to me."

His arms come back around me, but only for a quick squeeze, lingering a moment before he pulls away.

I'm so caught up in him that I'm not watching the waves. I guess Logan isn't either because all I hear is, "Oh shit!" before we're suddenly doused by white-water.

It knocks us apart and I come up sputtering and laughing. Logan immediately swims back over to me once he surfaces. "Shit, Daph, are you okay? Shit, I'm sorry."

"I'm fine," I laugh, pushing my wet hair out of my face. "Now see if you can catch me."

I start to swim away from him. He gives me a head start but then catches me in about three seconds anyway, and again, his amazing arms wrap around me.

Can I please stay in this ocean forever if it means he'll keep touching me like this?

But he says it's time for us to get out only fifteen minutes later, though I make him promise we'll go for another swim before we leave.

All I know is I never want the day to end. I want a lifetime of days on the beach with Logan Wulfe.

TWELVE

Present Day
Daphne

The next day, I knock softly at the oak paneled library door and wait. The light slanting in the hall is rich and bright. Late morning light. I slept until almost noon. But after last night, I needed it.

"Enter," comes the gruff invitation. My heart flutters and I push open the heavy door.

I'm naked, as ordered by a note left on my bedside table. My legs are shaky and my clit is sore, but I feel light. It's amazing to be able to wake up and have nothing to do but follow my Master's commands. And last night purged me of something, a heavy weight I'd been carrying. My guilt? Any last barriers between the girl I used to be and the woman I'm becoming?

All I know is that I want Logan more than ever. I want *this* more than ever. I want the man who takes me to the heights of pleasure and beyond, who knows me better than any other and who I can trust to take me even higher, darker, deeper. He'll never let me fall, and there's such a freedom in that like I've never known.

My gaze is naturally lowered as I pad barefoot through the shelves of leather-bound tomes. Master sits in a giant red velvet chair by the fire, a plate full of pastries on the Corinthian column pedestal table beside him. But where there used to be a matching red velvet chair and side table for me, there's only bare carpet.

Master snaps his fingers and points to a spot in front of him. That's when I see it: the large red tasseled cushion on the floor.

He expects me to kneel at his feet, lounging on the floor like a pet. Fuck. Warmth blooms in my lower belly. I'm turned on.

Master's face is cold and impassive, well, what I can see of it. He's wearing the mask and otherwise, he might as well be carved from marble.

He expects me to put up a fuss. To fight. A test?

I brush the shimmering fall of my hair from my face and lower myself gracefully to the floor. Surprise flickers across his face as I arrange myself on the cushion. Lest he think I'm a perfectly docile and obedient submissive, I shoot him a challenge through my lashes and raise a brow.

Long fingers steepled in front of his face, the Beast regards me. I'm so fascinated by this side of him. Strong. Dominant. Unyielding. Hot as fuck.

Anything could happen next and the thrill lighting up my chest makes me feel so fucking alive, like there's an undercurrent of electricity zinging through my bloodstream.

Still impassive, he breaks off a corner of a pastry. The

almond and vanilla scent makes my stomach roar. A corner of the Beast's mouth kicks up as he holds the sugar-dusted piece out to me.

But when I reach for it, he draws it back and tuts. *Fuck*. There's that bloom of humiliation, spreading across my cheeks, warming my pussy. Why does this turn me on? Screw it. I don't care why. I give into it.

Craning my neck, I open my mouth for the bite. The Beast places the pastry right in my mouth and taps my chin to signal his permission for me to eat. Blushing hot, I chew and swallow my breakfast, naked at Master's feet.

"Well done, pet," Master says, flicking crumbs off his fingers. *Pet*. My pussy clenches as he feeds me more bites. "You have a long way to go. But it's a start."

"So, I'm going to get clothes today?" I ask when my stomach is satisfied. I think I ask it more to challenge him than because I want them. It's the devil inside me. The same one that made me buy that red bikini at the beach that day so long ago. I've missed her.

"What makes you think you're entitled to them?"

"I thought I was earning back my company's patents, not the right to basic human privileges."

His fists clench when I mention the patents. "All your privileges will be earned. Remember, I control you. I own you."

Sensation stirs in my lower belly, a ripple of desire. To hide my reaction, I look to the fire. "But—"

Logan captures my chin and turns me to face him. "Careful. I have a lovely ball gag you could wear."

I wrinkle my nose. Would he really? Well, in for a patent, in for a pound. And anyway, if he did, would I...like it? The thing I've started to realize is that being submissive doesn't mean being docile.

If anything, it's allowing me to get in touch with my most base, animal self. If he gagged me, I'd snarl and roar and fight and he'd have to restrain me and maybe he'd clamp me again or do something else even more intense, maybe even pierce me, though I can't imagine an orgasm any more intense than yesterday's—

He chuckles, releasing me and distracting me from my tumultuous thoughts. "You think you have a choice. You have none. All your choices are mine." He snaps his fingers again, summoning me to a spot between his knees. "Now come. I wish to inspect you."

I raise my chin. "Why?"

His voice is a dangerous rumble. "It's enough that I wish it."

I can't forget who I'm playing with. Logan isn't just any Master. I rise and stand before him, my slender body braced by his powerful thighs. The stubble on his face is thicker today. Is he growing a beard? Trying to cover his scars? He's still wearing the mask. His shield. I miss his face. His icy blue eyes tell me nothing.

But the way he's rubbing his right thumb and forefinger together tells me everything. He wants to touch me.

The question is, why is he holding back?

"Turn around," he rasps. I pivot smoothly, tightening my muscles to still my trembling. Knowing that he wants me splashes gasoline on the fire of my arousal. The skin of my back and buttocks prickles as if his gaze is a caress.

"Hands and knees."

My heart drops to the carpet but I don't dare question him. What's in store today? I lower myself down to all fours.

His hand glides down my back and applies pressure to the center of my shoulders until I lower my front half to the floor. My cheek hits the scratchy Turkish rug. I study the rich red and navy pattern and try not to picture Logan leaning forward in his chair, peering straight at my pussy.

Except that's exactly what he does. Of course he does. The chair creaks and hot breath hits my buttocks. *Oh gods.* He's inspecting me. Thoroughly. Admiring his handiwork? The decorations the leather crop left on my skin? My sex spasms even at the memories.

By the time he put me to bed last night, I was so out of it, I barely remember him washing and rubbing cream into my sore bits. But I know he did. Though my body still bears some marks, the sting has faded. The lingering achiness is mostly from my muscles clenching as he teased me to the brink—and the cataclysm that was my orgasm.

An orgasm I sorely need. Again. I don't need the Scientific Method to tell me wherever Logan is concerned, I'm a simmering pot of arousal. Even when he's wielding evil clamps with metal teeth. His torture only turns me on a million times more. I had no idea I would or even *could* cum from so much pain.

Why? Maybe, on some level, I feel I deserve it? The pain is absolution, the pleasure a benediction. The punishment scours me clean. Enduring the trials, I earn what I need. But that's somehow...freeing. Even in humiliation and the pleasure it brings, I'm not embarrassed. I'm finally free.

"Reach back, pet, and spread your cheeks for me."

What?

I hesitate too long because Logan's tone drops a thousand degrees. "Did I not make myself clear?"

Shit! I wriggle my arms free and reach back, hissing as I grab a handful of tender flesh in each palm. But it's not the pain, it's the humiliation, knowing he's looking at me *right there*—

Something cool hits my asshole. And now he's *touching*

me, spreading what must be slippery lube all over the dark whorl of my back hole. He even probes the tight ring of muscle, making my lower belly flip with the *wrongness* of the sensation.

My hands release my cheeks and I squeeze them shut.

"Ahh, and you were doing so well." Logan murmurs. There's a rustle I don't have time to wonder about because I'm too busy stopping myself from running screaming from the room. I guess wallflower, hide-in-the-corner Daphne is still there inside me after all.

"Rise and face me," Logan orders in his deep Master voice.

Thank fuck. I shoot off the floor and whirl, sending my hair whipping over my front. Sure enough, Logan is holding a silver bulb with a generous amount of lube smeared at the tip.

"You were so pretty last night in your clamps, I've decided to add to your uniform." He tilts it and a hint of green winks from the base. "Green was always your color."

Of course he got me an emerald jeweled butt plug.

I swallow. I've never ever had anything up my butt. He promised it when I was here before, but we never got around to it...

Somehow I find my voice. It's squeaky but it works. "How many patents will you give me if I let you put that in?" I'm that girl on the beach. Brazen in her red bikini. Taking control of my own life. Of my own pleasure.

I'm not sure what's been happening these past few weeks, but I'm not letting go without a fight. Going back and having Adam steamroll over me...no, *letting* him steamroll over me. I can't be that girl anymore. I need to be someone new. It's time to grow the hell up.

But Logan's not about to let any defiance go unchallenged. He raises a thick brow. "Let me? Oh pet, you are mistaken. I won't be putting this in."

A rush of relief roars in my ears. Over the sound, I say, "No?"

"No. But it's going in." He sends me plummeting back to Earth. "Question is: will you insert it before or after your punishment?"

I DON'T KNOW how long I've been standing with my nose to the oak-paneled wall, staring at the honey grain. It feels like a lifetime. My ass throbs from the spanking Master gave me. My pussy is wet and my brain is torn.

Are my nipples hard from the cold or the humiliation of being told to stand in silence after punishment like a chastised child? Add to the indignity the unyielding metal butt plug stretching my virgin hole.

Behind me, paper flutters. Logan must be reading a paper, every so often turning the page. If he looked up he'd be able to see me standing in the corner, a statue with red marks on her ass and a sparkly green jewel between her butt cheeks.

When he made me put it in, I tossed it out at the first opportunity. He made me pick it up and clean it. Then he put me over his lap and inserted one size larger.

Then he spanked me and had me stand in the corner. The worst part isn't the pain. No. I can take way more. The worst part is my pussy's dying to be touched.

I clench my fists and fight the urge to sway from side to side. Any movement makes me more aware of the thick intruder in my ass.

"Stop fidgeting, pet." Another ripple of paper as he folds the newspaper.

I close my eyes and count my breaths, trying to relax but my ass feels strange with the huge invader stretching my back hole. So foreign. And so...*new*.

Every day, something new. Logan finds a new way to push me, to stretch my limits. I swallow a laugh. He is very literally stretching my limits today.

He paraded me in front of the mirror earlier so I could see in excruciating detail just how he's stretching me. That was right before he teased my clit and then sent me to the corner like a naughty schoolgirl.

Finally, finally, Logan orders me to turn around and beckons me to him. I take a step in his direction.

"No." His command slices the air. He snaps and points to the floor. "On your knees. Crawl to me."

Face on fire, I lower to all fours and crawl awkwardly across the carpet to him. My hair flops in my face. When the tips of his shoes come into view, I shuffle to a stop.

"We'll have to work on that."

And work on it we do. Over and over he makes me crawl back and forth until I'm grateful for the thick carpet. Back arched, head high, hips and breasts swaying as I slink across the room towards him. He has the crop again and uses it to guide my buttocks higher, my posture more sway-backed.

More and more I find my gaze slipping, fastening to the top button of his jeans. Round and dull as an ancient coin. Barely holding back the ever burgeoning length of his cock. He's not unaffected by my performance and that thrills me and pushes me on.

He didn't cum—not last night. Not today. Not yet. And it shows.

At last he sits, legs apart. "Now it's your turn to please me." This is a first. Ha. Today hasn't just been torture for me, has it? I feel like a cat presented with a bowl of cream.

The closer I get to Logan, the more I feel the intense heat emanating off his skin. As if his lungs are bellows and his heart a great hearth, pumping sparks and ash through his veins.

When I finally undo the button and zipper and palm his cock, it jumps in my hand. Little shocks of electricity run down my arms and spine. He's breathing hard but so am I. My cunt quickens as I breathe in his earthy scent.

My mouth waters but I force myself to sit back. "How many?" I ask, challenging him with my gaze.

His eyebrows shoot up. I'm on my knees before him, face level with his giant cock. The devil is back and she'll have her due. "How many patents does this earn?"

His eyes flash but he answers gruffly. "One. You should beg to please your Master."

I circle my fingers around his cock. A thick vein runs down the side. It pulses as I squeeze lightly. "Ten."

"Five."

I angle my head and blow along his length. My lips seek his testicles, brushing against the pebbled skin. I duck my head to hide my smirk. I've got him literally by the balls.

"Seven," I bargain back.

His jaw tightens and he glares down at me through his mask. It's cute, really, that he thinks it will put any barrier between us. He pretends to be so hard, so untouchable, but I know him. And yes, I let him master me, but I've begun to understand the reality of this power dynamic.

I have far more control than I first realized. Holy shit. I think... I think that's been part of what's been changing everything for me. It's not just sexual exploration. Number one, it's sexual exploration with Logan, the only man I could ever trust with my body this way. And number two, I've actually had so much more control than it appears from the outside. I'm the one who's been tied up, but I still have the power to hold this man captive.

Not that he's going to go down without a fight.

He places his foot between my legs. "You can sacrifice two of the seven patents in exchange for me letting you cum."

I whimper. Oooh, he fights dirty. But that's just part of the game. I grip him tighter and shift away from his foot. He denies himself all the time, and so can I.

"Seven," I say firmly, and then I drop my mouth over the head of his fat cock.

THIRTEEN

Present Day
Logan

Fuck. Oh fuck oh fuck oh *fuck*. Her mouth is on me. And then she fucking kills me by looking up with those luminous angel eyes and I almost cum right then and there.

Not that she's about to let me. She pulls back off with a loud, slurping *pop* and then her hands are massaging my inner thighs. Up to my balls. She grasps them and rolls them in her hand gently, then blows again right at the tip of my cock.

I can't help the shudder that works its way down my spine. I've been so controlled with her. So disciplined. A thousand times I've wanted to sink inside that golden pussy of hers.

This isn't exactly the same, but having my cock inside any part of her hot, wet, welcoming body is tantamount to torture. I should never have let her anywhere near…

But I can't bring myself to command her to stop. Just this once, it's okay. A master can enjoy his sub's attentions. That's part of the gig, right?

She licks an especially sensitive area right underneath the tip of my cock and my head drops backwards in my chair. Fuck, oh *fuck*.

My hips buck with her next tantalizing lick and I grip the armrests to try to control myself.

But shit, I can't let her know she's affecting me like this. "Suck it if you're going to suck it," I growl.

She looks up at me, raises an eyebrow, and then, while we're still locked in eye contact, she extends just the tip of her tongue and, back and forth, back and forth, lathes the very tip of my cock.

My hips jut forward again, desperate for more of her mouth, before my head can catch up. The head with a brain in it anyway. But it's too late. She's smiling a Cheshire's cat grin.

She pulls back altogether and moves back from me, still on her knees. "I want to show Master how well I've learned my lessons."

And then she crawls. She crawls in a circle on the rug, swaying her ass, her beautiful breasts bouncing as she puts herself on display for me. She's playing with me, teasing me. But when she finishes her circle and comes crawling back towards me, slinking like a lioness intent on her prey, fuck me but my cock goes harder than the hardest stone. My cock goes hard as a diamond.

My legs sag open wider at her approach. She gives an extra sway to her ass, sending her breasts jiggling as she reaches me and goes up on her knees, running her hands up from my knees to my upper thighs.

"I want to please my Master. I want to suck your cock and taste your cum down my throat."

My jaw hardens. My entire body flexes towards her. "Then please me."

And finally, *finally*, she grabs the base of my cock in one hand and then sinks her mouth on me again. I barely hold back my groan of relief.

But she's not holding back. Not anymore. She moans around me, the vibrations of her throat suctioned around my cock unlike anything I've ever felt before. I've fucking died. That's all I can think. I've fucking died and this is heaven, the woman I've always—

I cut the thought short. No more fucking thinking. Just take it for what it fucking is. Great head. I've got a slave who's great at giving head. Enjoy it. I'll sleep good tonight. That's all this is.

But then she reaches down, and the hand not at the base of my cock starts playing with my balls. My stomach heaves, I'm breathing so hard. She's driving me so fucking crazy.

I keep glancing down even though I tell myself not to. But the image of her on her knees is mesmerizing, her black hair cascading around her as she works and worships my cock so diligently.

I should hold out longer. Make her really work for it.

But then she looks up at me again. And she's still the sassy siren of a few minutes earlier who crawled towards me so confidently. But I also see a vulnerability there. Like she's wondering if she's doing it right. She looks like...she looks like *Daphne*.

She is the goddess who first woke me up to her womanhood when I saw her at the Ubeli's ball after her 18th birthday, who walked towards me on the beach on a day that is seared into my brain forever, like a siren in scraps of red fabric that I wanted to tear from her body. It all but killed me to act like a gentleman that day and for the months afterwards. She's the woman I spent hours talking late into the evening with, the person who I thought understood me better than anyone else.

I can't help reaching down a hand to cup her face. She closes her eyes and sinks against my hand even as she continues sucking me in and out, more vigorously than ever, like she wants me closer, deeper, *more*, her moans more frantic—

And I fucking lose it. I tap the side of her head but she doesn't move and I barely get the words out, "I'm cumming," but still she doesn't move away and then it's too late. I lose it and my hand tangles in her hair as my cum pumps out of me and paints the inside of her throat.

She swallows and sucks and swallows some more, her throat a vise around my cock, pulling even more cum out of me, and then more still.

I've never felt more empty or more complete and for a second, everything in the world is as it should be.

One breath. Two.

But then the real world comes buzzing back to life. Her warm mouth slips off of me. The cold intrudes. It's back to reality. And I've let her see too much.

She is who she is. The woman who betrayed me.

Or…did she? What if it was all a misunderstanding?

Says the guy who just got his brain sucked out through his dick.

I stand up abruptly and button my pants. "Good night, Daphne. You've earned your seven patents." And then I turn and go, not looking back once. Because I'm not sure I could bear seeing the hurt on her face.

FOURTEEN

Present Day
Logan

I sit in my study and try to focus on the academic journal I'm reading about nerve regeneration research but I've read the same fucking line at least ten times.

I slap the paper down on the floor beside my chair and stand, pacing in front of the fire. Having her under my roof again... I run my hands through my hair and imagine her up in her bed.

Her lithe little body curled up around her pillow. I remember the endless nights I watched her sleep after she caught cold from running headlong into the labyrinth.

Even then she was trying to escape you.

I laugh humorlessly and walk to the liquor cabinet, pour a couple fingers of whiskey, and down it. The fire bites at my throat but I'm already pouring another.

But I thought I could train her, make her mine. I

thought it meant something that she reached for me in her feverish dreams...but she was playing me even then. Planning her next escape from the second the first failed.

Did she think she could manipulate the patents out of me? Because I was so foolish to fall for her feminine wiles. That because I'm a disfigured recluse I would be easy to fool while she and that bastard Archer laughed themselves home to the bank?

And maybe now she's playing me all over again. I thought I knew her, but I've been substituting the memory of the girl that was for the woman that is now, and they aren't the same. Still, how many years did I long to have her in my arms? Of finally having the girl of my dreams?

And earlier, her angel lips around my cock, those paradoxically innocent fuck-me eyes... Sex with her is always more than just a master and sub. It's never so simple. That girl has so many hooks twisted up in my insides. A lifetime's worth.

But then I imagine her flashing *him* the same eyes. The betrayal burns so much deeper than her father's ever could. Just picturing her and Archer together, her laughing, curved into his body, her arms around his neck has me hurling the second glass of whiskey at the wall instead of drinking it.

Why am I still torturing myself like this? Why did I let her back into this house? Is it just because if she's *here* it means she's not *there* with him? That's what I told myself. That I'll never let them be together. That I'll ruin them both.

But then there was the way she's melted under my touch since she's been back. That wasn't acting. If sex is the only way to wring a genuine moment out of her...

Maybe I can't trust anything when it comes to her, though. All I know is I can't let her keep throwing me off balance like that. It's time to take back control, for my own fucking sanity.

My pacing suddenly leads me towards the door. I grab my mask and pull it on. And then I'm out of the office and stomping up the stairs.

To her room.

I don't bother being quiet as I slam the door open. Her yelp tells me she doesn't miss my lack of subtlety.

I don't turn on the lights as I head straight towards the bed. A small bit of light streams in from the window, just enough to make out the luscious shape of her body as she sits up in bed.

"Logan?" she asks, her voice thick with sleep and confusion. "What are y—"

"Silence," I bark.

I rip back the covers and her arms immediately move to cover herself. All she's wearing is a tiny camisole and panties. She's fucking gorgeous. A goddess. I grab her wrists and pin them over her head. Her chest heaves, perfect breasts round and nipples pebbling, and her eyes catch the light from the window, sparkling in the dark. Bewitching me all over again.

Which just fucking infuriates me. My teeth clench and I let go of her wrists only long enough to whip off my belt.

"Wait, Logan, I don't know if I can, not so soon after—"

"I said *silence!*" I hiss. I drop over her, getting right in her face. "Do you want to leave this bed, pack your bags, and get the hell out of my fucking castle? Then say so."

Her mouth purses like she's barely holding back from cursing me out and her hips buck underneath me.

But she doesn't say a word. I smile cruelly.

Then I take my belt, grab her wrists, and proceed to use it to tie her hands to the headboard.

The position exposes her breasts and makes them arch outwards. I can't help leaning over and drawing one into my mouth. She cries out again, but this time it's an ecstatic sound, and when she writhes underneath me, it's not to buck me off. She's melting. Already I know her body so well and it's a fucking high to feel her response.

But then it flashes through my mind like poison: the image of him on top of her, his hands on these perfect breasts.

And I bite down on her precious nipple.

"Logan!" she shouts, high and breathy, cumming hard.

My cock goes rock hard. The pain. She's orgasmed from the pain again. Oh *fuck*.

I lathe her nipple as she writhes underneath me and then I switch to the other, only letting up long enough to demand, "Do it again. Do it again now."

Then I suckle her other nipple to the point of pain, and, right as her writhing is at its most violent, I bite down again.

Again her moaning cries reach a fever pitch. "Logan, oh gods, Logan, *yes*, please. I— I lo—"

I slam a hand over her mouth as I raise up and straddle her, undoing the button of my fly. I straddle those perfect breasts and then order, "Silence."

Then I move my hand from her mouth to cover her eyes as I pull out my cock and begin to roughly stroke it. I'm wearing the mask but it only covers half my face and I'm too exposed. She can't see what she does to me.

Oh fuck, she's so beautiful tied up and laid out underneath me like a feast. She's still twisting and writhing, no doubt trying to get more friction on her clit or her breasts but she won't find either.

Though that doesn't mean I won't tease her with what

she won't ever have again. I press my cock between the valley of her luscious breasts.

And almost pass out from the filthy fucking picture it makes.

I have to defile her smooth, blemish free skin. I have to mark her as fucking mine. I fist my cock painfully and drag up and down. I grab my balls roughly and squeeze, then go back to stroking myself.

"Please, Logan, I want to see," she whimpers.

"Quiet," I growl, one hand still firmly in place over her eyes. She'll never see me vulnerable like this. But I still have to mark her. I've never felt a more carnal drive in my whole fucking life.

"No, fuck quiet," I suddenly decide. "Beg me," I demand. "Beg to be painted in my cum."

She swallows hard and a shudder runs through her body. "Please Logan. I- I want your cum. I want every part of you. I want to feel your cum on my tits. I- I need it. I want to feel you spurt so hot on me. I want you to rub it in and claim me—"

"Oh fuck," I groan and I can't hold it back any more.

"Logan, make me dirty with your cum—"

Cum jets out of my cock so hard it splatters all over her tits and into the hollow of her throat. Her back arches and she thrusts her breasts out to receive even more of my cum, which just keeps shooting out in the most powerful fucking spurts I've ever experienced.

And then I do just as she begged. I rub it into every inch of her breasts, massaging and marking her with my cum like it's the most expensive lotion.

When I'm done, we're both panting like we've run a marathon.

I want to collapse on top of her. I want to hold her to

me. I remember the one and only night we spent together back when she was really my girl. Or at least back before the world had corrupted her.

Maybe she was always this...this deceitful thing, and I just couldn't see it back then. But no, she was just a young woman in pain. I truly don't believe there was malice in her back then. Although I don't know if I can even trust myself anymore. Everything I thought I knew... I was such a fool, so blindsided by what was to come.

But for awhile, I thought I could still hold everything together. Her father's company. *Her*. I thought we could make it, that I could be strong enough for all of us.

She blinks up at me in the darkness, those luminous eyes that I so long mistook for soul-searching. I break her gaze and roughly undo her wrists. "Get your beauty sleep. You'll need it, considering what I have planned for you tomorrow."

FIFTEEN

7 Years Ago
Daphne

"Wake up, sleepy kitten," Logan's gently teasing voice wakes me. "We're home."

I blink open my eyes. We went for another beach outing, something we've done several times this summer, even though it's not even technically summer anymore. September's just begun but that meant the beaches were less populated.

Logan and I swam in the ocean like we always do, my favorite part since it's an excuse for him to sometimes put his hands on me. Like an idiot, I live for those touches.

But things have been so bad at home that I was especially eager for the escape today. Because I'm a terrible person. Eager to leave her ill mother and worried, moody, anxious father... But Mom told me to go, said she'd be angry if I didn't.

And the day on the golden sand, stretched out beside Logan, counting the freckles on his arm and dreaming up new constellations from the way they're arranged while the waves crashed in the background and the sun warmed my skin...*heaven*.

My whole body is still relaxed from the day as I sit up in the truck, still sleepy. "What time is it?" I reach for my phone only to find it's run out of battery.

"About nine o'clock."

"Wow." I scrub my face, the smell of salt and sand permeating Logan's truck. "Sorry to just conk out on you like that."

He smiles sideways at me as he pulls into the driveway in front of Thornhill. "Don't be. You're angelic when you sleep."

His eyes linger on me and the intensity that seems to occasionally spark between us lights up like a firecracker in the small space of the cab.

I want to reach out and touch his face. I want to climb his body like I did in the ocean when I pretended to be afraid of something in the water even though I knew it was really just seaweed catching at my feet.

I want to ask him if it really is just obligation that's had him spending so much time with me or if it's something else, if he sees me like a man sees a woman. If there could ever be something between us or if I'm going to be doomed to this hopeless longing forever.

But the moment is suddenly broken when the front door of Thornhill crashes open, slamming against the wooden frame of the house, and my father storms out.

"Where the *hell* have you been?" he shouts.

I stumble out of the truck. "Daddy, I'm so sorry, what's going on?"

And…that's when I realize he's not talking to me at all. It's Logan he's shouting at. "My wife is *dying* and you have your cell phone turned off all day? What the hell is wrong with you?"

Dad gets right up in Logan's face. "She's turned and could be a matter of *days* if we don't save her now and you're off gallivanting with—"

A matter of days? *Oh Mama.*

Then Dad's eyes turn disdainfully my way, looking me up and down. "And you would just abandon your mother like that? I thought I raised you to be a better daughter."

His words cut to the quick and I flee towards the house.

"Daphne!" Logan calls after me but I don't turn to look back. I have to see Mom. *A matter of days*. And I missed one of them, at the beach, being one of those idiot girls I hate, stupid about a boy who doesn't even like me back.

Tears are rolling down my cheeks by the time I make it to Mom's room.

And she does look worse than when I left her this morning. She's got an oxygen mask on and her skin, it doesn't look right. It seems papery and gray and like the veins are too close to the surface.

"Mama!" I cry, rushing to her bedside and crashing to my knees beside it, taking her hand. Her eyes are sunken and they move slow, like it takes her effort to even move them to look at me.

"I'm so sorry I wasn't here!"

But she shakes her head and motions for me to remove her oxygen mask.

"You need it."

She frowns at me in that demanding way that is so Mom, I smile through my tears and do as she asks.

Her eyes soften but she looks so tired, a frail shell of her former beauty. "I'm glad," her voice comes out a frail whisper. "I'm glad you went. Too much of your life," she takes a heaving breath, "in this sick room."

"No, Mom, all I want is to be with you." More tears well and spill down my cheeks. Please, the last thing I want her to think is that she's a burden. "You're the best part of my life."

She smiles at that and then lifts a wan hand to run through my hair. "A mother's job is to send her daughter out into the world. To see her happy." A big, heaving breath. "Not to hold her back like your father and I have all these years."

I shake my head fervently. "You haven't held me back. I've been *so* happy."

"You will be. You *will* be. Live your life. For me. Swear you will. Swear it."

I nod, trying to swallow back tears. "I swear."

"Good," she breathes out. "Because I want you to spend every day at the beach. To fall in love a hundred times. Or maybe just once with the right man."

I can't help lowering my eyes as my cheeks flush.

Mom squeezes my hand. "Oh darling. Logan?"

I open my mouth to tell her it's just a stupid crush but when I look up, she's beaming at me. "He's a good man. And I see the way he looks at you. Like you hang the moon and stars."

And then she relaxes back into the bed, her eyes closing. I suspect it's taken more effort than I thought for her to say so much, but still she whispers. "I'm so glad. You'll need someone strong to look out for you when I'm gone."

I shake my head and start to chide her for negative thinking, but only her gentle snores meet me. She's fallen asleep.

Her hand is cold in mine and when I feel along her arm and her feet, her entire body is cold. So I climb in bed beside her and nestle in behind her, chafing her arms lightly to warm her up.

"Everything's going to be okay, Mama," I whisper, terrified I don't believe my own words. "Everything's going to be okay. Daddy's going to fix you, just you wait and see."

But the next morning, when I wake up, it's to the loud buzzing of machines alerting of a problem.

And my mother is cold in my arms.

Dead and gone from this world.

SIXTEEN

Present Day
Daphne

A huge dark shape moves over me in the darkness, then settles behind me, grabbing both of my wrists in one strong hand and holding them at the small of my back.

"Surrender," he murmurs, his cock gliding along my fingers and then settling in the cleft between my legs. He is a wall of heat behind me as his body weight settles into the mattress. His cock a hard, unyielding promise. My hands fist but my bottom rises to meet his thrusts. "Let go. Let yourself be mine. Every part of you. Don't hold a single part back."

"Logan," I whisper. I flex my fingers and he releases my wrists, but only so he can guide them over my head where he takes hold of them again.

But not before a dark glint catches my eye. The ring is a weight heavy on my finger. Not a diamond, though. A signet ring crowned with a gold beast's head. The mark of his claim. My heart soars at the sight.

Logan threads his thick fingers with my small ones, covering my hand with his. In the dark, my lips curve.

"I was always yours."

My eyes snap open and the sun hits me in the face. My pussy's tight and aching, my hips rocking towards the ceiling. I breathe out in frustration, so turned on from my dream it must have freaking woke me *up*.

And no wonder. I look down at myself and my breath hitches again. I'm still covered in Logan's cum. Was it only last night? He barged in here, made me beg and then...

I turn and bury my face in the pillow, wishing I could have stayed in the dream a little longer. Maybe in that dream world he would have eventually let me touch him. Maybe even wrapped his arms around me like he did that one night...after the funeral, when I felt more alone than I ever had before in my life.

But then Logan came.

I blink and lay on my side, staring at the sun pouring in the eastern window. For once in my life, there's no rush to be anywhere. No lab tests, no meetings, no board breathing down my neck.

No inconvenient fiancés.

Still not getting out of bed, I reach over and pull out the bedside table drawer. The diamond flashes at me from the engagement ring. I pulled it off and tossed it in there as soon as I could, along with my phone.

Tethers to my old life, which feels increasingly far away. If only I could walk away forever, wave a wand and have all my responsibilities disappear.

The old Daphne would never feel this way. But...is that necessarily a bad thing?

I shove the drawer shut. I was going to call my dad, check in, but I'm not in the mood. The last few times I've called, he's been asleep or busy with PT anyway. I can call him later and it'll be fine. And I can pretend this is my life—a simple existence as Logan's plaything—a little longer.

If I stop and think too hard, I know nothing about this is simple. And yet it is at the same time.

I close my eyes and will the dream to continue.

His arms around me.

But it's not a dream that plays behind my eyelids. It's the memories again. Memories I can't escape, that somehow feel so fresh it's as if it all happened last night.

His arms around me that terrible night, comforting me as I wept for my mother. How safe and cherished he made me feel. I think... I think that was the last time I ever felt that until... until now. Until he came back into my life.

First with my mom's death and then his disappearance out of nowhere. Everything just sort of...*stopped.*

I just...stopped.

Emotionally and as a person, all the gears inside me slowed down and came to a grinding halt.

I was hurting so bad and there was no one there to help me understand or figure out how to get through it. Certainly not my father.

I frown and finally roll out of bed, heading for the shower.

The shower spray is cleansing hot. I wash, rinse, and rewash my hair several times, and survey the marks on my body. Mostly faded. Will Logan give me more today? *Please, Master, will you whip me again?* My laugh echoes around the luxuriously tiled room.

Dear gods, what is my life?

Because the thing is, while I might have been frozen in

amber at 19, now at 27, I am waking the fuck back up. In a completely full-grown woman's body.

I get out and blow-dry my hair, taking the time to style it. The woman in the mirror is a sloe-eyed seductress. I pucker my lips and she blows me a kiss.

Have I ever done this? Enjoyed a lazy morning, primping in the bathroom? Surely there was a moment in my teens when I posed for the mirror, figuring out how to get my hair to fall in sultry waves just so.

I wrack my brain but there's no memory of happy time to myself. My teen years were dedicated to school, research, taking care of my mom. No fun with girlfriends. Not even a sleepover.

Not that I regret it. But, other than being the youngest recipient of the Avicennius grant, and a straight A student, and a dutiful daughter, who was I then?

Who am I now?

I run the brush through my hair. The woman in the mirror looks more serious now, but still calm. Of course she is. She doesn't have a schedule. She has nothing to do but look beautiful and follow Master's commands.

I envy her.

It could be like this forever.

I grip the edge of the countertop. No, I can't think that. Is that what I want? To be Logan's slave? His plaything?

But I'm more than a plaything. Isn't that what I just realized? It's not a one-way street.

I look myself in the mirror and I'm finally honest with myself: I'm not here for the patents. Whatever Logan's motives, I'm here because I got a taste of being awake and alive, and I can't go back.

Was your old life so much better anyway? The beauty in the mirror looks me straight in the eye. *Well? Was it?*

A company on the brink of collapse. A father who loves me only as an extension of his own scientific accomplishments. A fiancé I never wanted.

Still, it's not like I can just give all that up, can I? Walk away from my responsibilities?

Were they your responsibilities in the first place? Was it your life? Your choice?

Yes. Everything I worked for, everything I was—I wanted. My heart starts beating quicker at all the rebellious thoughts. Right?

A sharp knock has me scurrying out of the bathroom. By the time I open the door, Logan is gone. Either that, or little elves delivered a cart with a silver, covered breakfast tray to my door. I roll the cart inside, my stomach clenching at the smell of bacon.

When I remove the cover, a note falls to the floor. My daily instructions.

After you eat, open the box by your bed.

I'm too curious to wait. Munching on a strip of bacon, I head to the bedside table where, sure enough, Logan left a plain black box, a bit bigger than the kind fancy chocolates might come in. It could hold anything.

As soon as I open it and see the gleaming metal, I know. My stomach swoops and my heart starts to beat faster.

Each butt plug is numbered strangely. 11:00-12:00. 13:00-14:00. 15:00-16:00. And the largest: 19:00. Times of the day, I realize. I'm to wear each one for an hour, graduating in size. This is my only task for the day.

Under the box is a final note. *Meet me in the dungeon at 19:30.*

The dungeon. *Unf.* My pussy clenches. I pick up the smallest butt plug and grimace at my distorted reflection.

But it's immediately followed by a thrill of excitement.

Tonight, Logan claims all of me.

HE LEFT a final note with further instructions with my lunch. I could walk down the stairs to the dungeon. But as soon as I passed through the heavy doors, I had to crawl.

But he laid out a carpet. Red. Strewn with rose petals.

A second before I cross the threshold, I drop to my knees. I can't describe what it feels like, the dirty thrill I feel at lowering myself to the ground. It's dirty and sexy and when I crawl seductively, I can feel his eyes on me almost like a physical thing. Can he see the large plug in my ass from this angle? Gods, I never knew there could be such power in being on my knees.

I crawl until Logan's feet come into view. They're bare, roped with veins and dusted with dark hair. He's seated on a huge throne-like chair, the grandly carved wood dark with age. A king in his castle.

I settle myself on my knees before him and wait. Seconds tick by like years.

"Did you follow my instructions like a good girl?" His voice is a throaty growl.

I dare then to look up. "Yes, Master."

His eyes gleam. "Up." He indicates the table in the center of the room. With a shaky sigh, I rise and climb onto the leather-padded top. Sitting like a patient waiting for a doctor, bare ass naked.

Except this patient has a huge butt plug stretching her sphincter. I subtly lean on one hip.

"On your back," Logan orders, and leaves his throne to collect items from a cabinet.

Deep breath. I lay back and try to relax. As if this is a pap smear or some sort of similar torture.

Sessions with Logan have a big advantage over a regular doctor's visit, though. There's more pain, but way more chance of orgasms.

I school my face into a blank expression as Logan returns, rolling some sort of cart with him. His shadow falls over me and my leg twitches. I shift on the table, trying to get comfortable with the biggest butt plug I've ever worn stuffed inside me. I might not know what's coming, but that's always been part of the thrill, hasn't it?

"Do I need to tie you down?" Logan rasps when I shift again.

"No. I trust you." I give him a nervous smile.

Nothing. He's still wearing the mask. A black one tonight. With his silk shirt and slacks, he's a thin mustache away from sexy Zorro.

And now I want to smile. I must be nervous. That's why I'm making bad jokes, even if just in my head.

But the thing is, I meant what I just said. I do trust him, in spite of everything that's happened. He's never betrayed or hurt me. So I take a deep breath and still all my twitching limbs.

"Since you wore the nipple clamps so well." He holds up a tiny jeweled ornament. Similar emeralds, but no clamp attached. It takes me a second to recognize what it is and when I do, the breath leaves my body.

Oh shit, he's going to pierce me.

This is permanent.

"No comment?" he smirks at me. I shake my head slowly.

If this is what he wants, then I want it too.

Is it really that easy? Has it really been that easy all

along? All I needed to come alive again this whole time, to find my freedom— the solution was never to clench tighter and try to control things like my life was a series of scientific labs steps to follow.

What I didn't know, what I could never know without Logan coming back into my life and showing me, was that the truest freedom can only be found in ultimate surrender.

I don't tell him this. Instead, I let my body sink into the table as he briskly brushes antiseptic over my nipples. The sharp, clean scent stings my nose. The act is supremely erotic. The silence, the slight tickle of the brush. The care Master takes with his slave. My breathing deepens, my body slipping into that submissive state, readying me for what's to come.

I feel like a new creature. Like my life is just beginning.

"You told me you liked pain. That it made you feel alive." Logan's voice is level, but his fingers tremble slightly as they pass over my breast. Even without me saying it, he knows something of what I'm feeling. That's how attuned we are.

"It does. I do." I raise my chin. "Give me the rose with the thorns."

He turns back to bend over the tray, but his cheek curves. "Leave it to you to see the beauty in pain."

"The way I see it, life is equal parts hurt and love. If I numb myself to one, then I miss out on the other."

"You speak as though you've had a lifetime of suffering."

Silently I tally up everything I've been through. My mother's death, my father's grief. The illnesses that have shaped my entire life. My own striving for love. "I'm not saying I'm the only one who's suffered. Or that I've suffered more than most."

Logan remains silent and I keep babbling. I feel like I'm

having such huge revelations and I want to share some of it with him.

"Socrates says if all the world's suffering was laid in a pile, most people would choose their own portion. I wouldn't change my life for anyone else's. But I've been numb for too long." I lock eyes with him. "I'm ready to be awake to my life. Even for the parts of it that hurt."

He doesn't say anything for a long moment. He just stands there, ice blue gaze searing straight into my soul.

Then suddenly he starts stripping out of his shirt and my mouth goes dry. Crossing the room to a sink, he washes his hands, then returns to show me the needle.

I can't stop my smile. "I'm not afraid of needles." I've encountered enough in my lifetime.

He shakes his head and starts to sterilize the needle. "This will earn you twenty patents," he says gruffly, still turned away from me. The muscles of his back are as chiseled as the stone walls of his castle.

When he comes to my side, I grab his hand. "No." He is missing the whole point.

His nostrils flare and his gaze is a blade. "This is happening, Daphne."

I drop my hand and soften my voice. "That's not what I meant. You don't have to give up patents for this. I want it." I want *you*. But I'm not quite brave enough to say that yet.

For a moment he's frozen except for a slight widening of his eyes. The blue of his iris is a thin circle of ice. Then, in a growl, "What game are you playing?"

"No games. Not any more. I want to do this."

"No patents?" The furrow between his brows is etched deep, he's so confused.

"No."

He stares at me a long moment. *See me,* I plead silently. *See us. What we could become.*

"This doesn't change anything," he says, and pinches my nipple in preparation. I watch him, not the needle, as if I could communicate everything I'm thinking telepathically.

I want this. I'll do anything...for you.

Because it's true, I want to be awake. I don't want to be numb or frozen anymore. But there's more to it than that. I wouldn't have woken up to just anyone. I want the man in front of me. My first crush. My first love. I want it all, with him.

I'm a silent observer as Logan bends over me. I see him and the room as if I'm a ghost by the ceiling. A young woman prone on the table, her hair spread in a dark halo around her head.

The pinch, when it comes, feels far away. Logan adorns my left nipple with a tiny barbell with green jewels. His eyebrows are furrowed again, but this time in concentration. Then he sterilizes everything and repeats the process with my right.

He lets the needle clatter onto the tray. "It's done."

I come back into my body, sucking air into my lungs. My nipples throb. But so does my clit. My full ass only emphasizes how my pussy is empty.

Logan examines me thoughtfully. His fingers come to my cunt and slide inside. "Wet," he says hoarsely.

I stare at him as if I can see past the mask. "Always." *For you.*

He presses a button and the table starts to lower. I jolt. Now what?

He kneels and tugs my legs down, dragging me to the edge of the table until I'm straddling his face.

I rise up on my elbows. "Wha—?"

"You've earned this." His voice is muffled between my thighs.

The mask is cool when it touches my skin. Soon it's slick with my juices. I grab his hair and cant my hips, rocking into his mouth.

"That's it, baby. Grind it out." He angles his head and probes my pussy with his tongue. A minute more and it's too much. My toes scrunch and I cum, screaming.

He rises over me, his chin and mask shiny. Grabbing his shirt, he mops his face.

I lie back, insides still quivering. The pain in my nipples is a million miles away. "How many?" I gasp.

He raises a brow.

"How many patents did I give up in exchange for that orgasm?"

He licks his lips, which are glossy with my essence. "None."

My heart stops for a second. I smile, and he returns it. Just a small quirk beside his lips, a tiny parentheses, but it's enough.

This doesn't change anything, he'd told me. In that moment, we both know he's wrong.

SEVENTEEN

Present Day
Logan

She lies on the table, her body a delectable offering to a cruel god. Green jewels sparkle at the reddened tips of her breasts, the tan cleft of her ass.

She spent the day training her ass for me, stretching it until she crawled in here with a plug so large it pushes her ass cheeks apart. It's got to be uncomfortable, but when I twist and tug on it, her pussy weeps. Her juices drench my hand. Needy little thing.

Needy enough not to want patents in exchange for what we just did. Is this just some new game? Another way for her to manipulate me?

I frown briefly even as her eyes smile sleepily at me. I drop my hand. "You should rest."

"No," her voice rings out. "You need to claim all of me."

"You want me to fuck your ass?" My hand returns to the

plug, pushing and pulling to make it stretch her back hole. My cock strains against my zipper.

"You promised."

"I did no such thing."

"You implied." Her eyes flash indignation. *I trained my ass all afternoon long...for this?*

I pull on the butt plug, drawing it out of her. Her middle tenses and she sighs when I push it back in. Oh, she wants it all right. She's not faking that.

"I won't be gentle," I warn. She doesn't get to tease the beast without consequences. Which she well knows.

"I can take it." She's confident. Still, her eyes widen when I shuck off my jeans. My cock is thick and pulsing. I grab her right hand and bring it to my cock. Her slender fingers barely fit around my monster dick. Did she forget so soon how big I am?

I grit my teeth as she jacks me, and my toes curl into the stone floor. Fuck, her touch feels so good. I want to grab her and fuck her hard. To finally be inside her body again. Her eyes are so welcoming. Her skin flushed. Her pussy weeping its juices for me. My hips jut forward towards her hips, needing contact even as something else inside me clenches, holding back.

"Can you, Daphne? Take all of me?" My voice comes out harsh. Almost cruel.

Daphne's not affected in the least. Eyes hooded, she only tries to reach for me with her left hand, but I pin it back in place.

Control. I have to stay in control.

I thread a hand in her hair and bring her to her knees before me.

"Suck me," I bark. I widen my stance and my cock bobs in front of her face. "Make it good."

She opens her mouth and swallows the head of my cock eagerly. Too eagerly. Halfway onto my dick, she chokes, her eyes watering. I loosen my grip, allowing her to control her own movements. She pulls off and gasps, but forces herself back onto my cock, gobbling me down like a starving woman at a feast. I hit the back of her throat, and she gags, but keeps fighting to stay on.

"Oh, fuck, Daphne. Fuck me." I cradle her face. Tears stream down her cheeks, a black river of mascara, but she doesn't quit. Her hands massage my thighs.

"Look at me," I order, and she does. Wide, green eyes, wet with tears but still hungry. Desperate with need and... desperate to please me, too. Fuck, what is she doing to me? Besides turning my world upside down. I want to push her. I want to punish her. I want to make love to her.

Her head bobs frantically and she gains another few centimeters with each pass. I hold her a moment on my dick and then let her back off to catch her breath.

"Back up. On the table. Hold yourself open and offer yourself to me." I lost this war before it even began.

She scrambles up and kneels on the low table. Face down, hands on either ass cheek, tugging them apart. The butt plug fills her tiny hole. I draw it out and watch the stretched skin retract. My cock throbs so hard I almost black out. *Fuck me.*

I have to have her. Now. I grab a bottle of lube and slick up my cock. If I touch her beautiful golden skin too soon...

"Fuck me, Daphne," I breathe as I line up my cock with her back hole. Her anus has shrunk without the plug, and I push inside before she tightens up even more. My entire body shutters with first contact and I'm glad she's facing away from me and can't see.

The head of my cock breaches the first tight ring of

muscle. She wriggles a little, helping me work in further and oh fuck oh fuck oh *fuck*. I almost lose my mind. Her channel squeezes me tight and all the blood rushes from my head to my dick. I steady myself, my hands huge on her tiny, tapered waist.

Every time I have my hands on her, it feels like the most natural thing on earth. In a world full of wrong, here, finally, is something *right*.

And then the terrible, wonderful thought strikes me: *What if she's real?*

What if she's really my girl? What if she really is the girl next door that I met all those years ago? That girl at the beach who walked out in the red bikini and scalded my eyes. The girl I could talk to for hours. The woman I gave her first kiss, her first orgasm, the only woman I've ever— What if she's real? The innocent and the sex pot and the perfect and imperfect, all wrapped up together in the marvelous package laid before me, wanting me for nothing else other than *me*?

Her hair cascades down her back, slipping off when she tries to turn her head. What does she see? A monster, a giant beast impaling her on his impossibly big rod? I ease further inside her and fall forward, covering her body with mine. I'm wedged tight inside her, dying to fuck, but I want to feel her, gather her trembling form into my arms.

I kiss her between her shoulder blades but the smooth, false skin of my mask is still a barrier between us.

"Eyes front." I tug on her hair to enforce the order. The thought that she might be my fantasy made reality is too much, but like a fool, I still want it. I'm also tempted by the vision, and with her body wrapped around me, I'm lost in her. Finally inside her again, I can't bear any more barriers between us. Even if it makes me the biggest fool in the universe.

But when she's facing forward again, I rip off the mask and toss it to the corner. Then I grasp her hips and slide her back onto my cock, making her groan as I conquer her ass. Her channel squeezes me so tightly I'm afraid my dick will snap off. I rock gently and lights flash in the corner of my eyes. The lube eases my entry, but in this moment, I just need to fuck her. I need to claim what's mine. I want to hold on to possibility. And I want her to feel me so far into next week that she knows who her Master is.

My orgasm gathers in the base of my spine. She's passive under me, grunting softly as I ream her ass. A perverse part of me loves that she's uncomfortable. But I also want to make her cum. Watch her fall apart while I'm balls deep inside her ass. Make her love the depraved things I do to her body. Make her crave them. Make her crave me.

Next time, I'll train her ass myself, and force her to cum only when the plug is wedged tight in her bowels. I want to do such filthy, wrong things to her and I want to make her love them.

I reach my hand under her and, sure enough, she's a sopping mess. Poor, neglected pussy. I find her clit and grind the heel of my palm against it, making her cry out. My free hand grabs a handful of her hair, drawing her head back as I pummel her bottom. I want to hurt, to destroy her. Break her down until she's in pieces. Then rebuild. She'll be reborn. I'll make her new. Make her mine.

A roar builds in my throat. Daphne cums with a howl, my hand at her clit and cock in her ass. She shudders hard, her back bowing until I'm afraid she'll break in two. Her ass clenches around me, ripping out my cum. I fill her to the brim with my creamy offering, then pull out and coat her perfect ass.

Then I lean on the table, trembling, weak from my orgasm. The mask glimmers in the corner, empty eyes pointed in our direction, a judgmental voyeur. My clothes are crumpled on the floor. I left pieces of me all over the room.

Because, this night and always, Daphne's the one who broke me apart.

She's destroyed me. And I'm the one reborn.

Daphne

I THOUGHT it might mean something: giving myself over completely. But when I go to turn around and hug my Master, he stops me. A dark cloth drops over my face. He blindfolds me carefully, and leads me from the dungeon. Rose petals whisper at my feet.

Logan is gentle as he guides me to the bathroom, to a shower first for a rinse and then a tub full of fragrant water. Judging from the soft fluttering against my bare skin, he's added rose petals. He eases me back and washes me gently, taking care not to disturb or submerge my newly pierced nipples.

But he won't let me touch him. When I reach for him, he captures my wrists.

"No," he rasps.

"But..." I bite my lip. We just shared a moment, I know we did, but he's holding back. Retreating behind his stone walls. I opened myself completely, but it wasn't enough to earn his trust.

I fight back tears as he takes me from the tub and dries me off. He removes my blindfold so I can take out my contacts. But his mask is back, firmly in place. I finish my business in the bathroom and head to bed where he waits for me in the darkness.

"I want to see you," I whisper as he draws up the covers, tucking me in.

"I know." His lips are on my forehead. The mask is cool on my skin. And I hate it. I hate how he hides. Not because he's holding back from me, but because he thinks he's ugly. The mask is a shield, but it hasn't stopped me from hurting him.

He retreats to the door, pausing when I call his name.

"How, Logan? How can I earn *you?*"

He pauses and my silly heart fills to the brim with hope.

"You can't."

And when he leaves, I feel nothing but despair.

EIGHTEEN

7 Years Ago
Daphne

My whole life has been spent towards one goal: saving my mother from death by this horrific disease.

And I failed.

I didn't grow up fast enough, finish my degree quick enough, spend enough time with her while I had her on this earth.

And now she's gone.

Gone.

It's not fair. I believed *so hard* we would save her. That if I just did everything I was supposed to and worked hard enough…

But I've been a little naïve fool, imagining there's any order or balance or fairness to things in the universe at all.

I've been a child still believing in fairy tales.

It rains while they lower my mother into the ground

beneath an angelic statue at Thornhill. The heavens weep along with me and my father.

The entire community would have been here, but my father refused anyone beyond the priest, Logan and Adam, a few others from the research lab, and me.

I don't have any friends here, other than Logan, but he's standing under an umbrella beside my father, though his eyes keep coming to me.

I don't care. I don't deserve to be comforted. I failed her. I deserve every ounce of chill and cold and hurt and—

I hiccup as a fresh round of tears hits me.

A woman I barely know from Dad's lab comes over and tries to put an arm around my shoulder but I pull away.

They've finished putting Mom in the ground and I rush forward and throw a single bright red rose on top of the casket. Her favorite.

And then I turn and flee back towards Thornhill, abandoning the umbrella about halfway there and letting the rain lash my face the rest of the way.

I'm cold to the bone as soon as I yank open the heavy wooden front door and I'm breathing hard as I slam it shut again. I flee upstairs to my bedroom.

I slam that door, too, and shove rain-soaked hair out of my face as I start to yank at the collar of the stifling black dress, when I see it—on my white, virginal bedspread—a single red rose.

Just like the one I put on Mama's casket. A crimson Heathcliff. Her favorite.

I slink out of the heavy, soaked dress so that I'm just in my silk camisole and slip and curl onto the bed, clutching the rose and fingering the delicate petals.

Who put it here?

It feels like a sign from my mother. A reminder of beauty and goodness when all I feel is pain.

There's a knock at the door and I sit up. Did Dad actually come after me? Did he put the rose here? He's barely tried to comfort me since she died. Hasn't even tried to hug me. Is this his way of reaching out?

"Come in."

But it's not Dad who pushes open the door.

It's Logan.

The disappointment at it not being Dad is only momentary because I immediately feel a rush of gratitude that Logan *did* come. Of course he noticed me leaving the funeral. Of course he came. He's Logan.

He only proves the point when he nods towards the rose. "Looks like someone remembered the birthday girl."

I look down at the rose in surprise. Oh my— He's right. It's my birthday. I'm nineteen now. On the day I buried my mother.

I double over as fresh rounds of sobs rack my body.

"Oh, hey, hey," he says, immediately coming over and wrapping his big, warm arms around me. "Shhh, it's going to be okay."

But I shake my head. "No, no it's not. That's just something people say. But it's a lie. Nothing's ever going to be okay again. Not when—" I hiccup. "Not without Mom."

He holds me tighter and I twist in his arms, burying my head in his warm chest.

And he holds me as I sob out my pain.

"Ouch," I yelp as I shift several minutes later.

"What?" Logan pulls back, immediately alarmed.

I hold up a finger, pricked by one of the rose's thorns, welling with bright red blood.

Logan grabs my hand and immediately brings it to his

mouth, sucking on the finger. I don't think he quite realized what he was doing, it was just an instinctual reaction.

But then, as if it hits him that he's sitting on my bed with my finger in his mouth, suddenly his eyes darken as they lock on to mine.

And suddenly all I can think of is Mom making me swear that I'd live my life. Live the life that she couldn't.

And all reason and sanity take a flying leap out the window.

I pull my finger from Logan's mouth and pounce on him, wrapping my arms around his neck and trying to land my mouth on his.

But I'm not fast enough.

He shakes his head and grabs my cheeks, holding me back.

His chest heaves as he presses his forehead to mine. "I won't take advantage of you, Daph. You're grieving right now. You're not in your right mind."

Which is just fucking infuriating. Because maybe he's a little bit right, but I still know what I want. "I want you, Logan." It comes out pleading and breathy, but it's also one of the most honest things I've ever uttered in my entire life.

I've all but crawled in his lap and one hand moves from my face to curl around my waist as he drops his head to the crook of my neck.

"Don't do this to me, Daph. Not right now. I can't be another person close to you who lets you down when you need them the most."

For a second, we just sit like that, me half on top of him and him clutching me like I'm a lifeline.

But then—and I swear I can feel his entire body shaking —he takes me by my waist and sets me off him.

The tears start up again the second I lose contact. "I've

ruined it," I whisper. "You're going to leave now and I'll never see you again."

He pauses from where he's standing beside the bed and runs a hand through his hair. "Your Dad wants me back in the lab right away…"

I nod and turn my face away from him. I must seem so pathetic. So sad and piteous, trying to kiss him and expecting him to feel anything back. Sad, pathetic—

But then I feel a weight on the bed behind me as the mattress dips.

"Daph, when was the last time you slept?" His voice is so gentle, it only makes it worse.

"Not since—" I hiccup when I try to breathe. "Not since the morning when I woke up and found her—"

"Fuck," he swears under his breath, "Daph, that was days ago."

There's more movement behind me. "Come here."

He pulls back the blankets and then he pulls me into him, my back to his front, and his heavy, masculine arm curls around my waist. "I've got you," he murmurs into my hair. "Just sleep, baby. Just sleep."

I'm already dreaming, is the last thought I have before I drift off.

NINETEEN

Present Day
Logan

The moon is a cold coin, glowing silver in a starless sky. I raise a glass of whiskey and drain it in one go. Midnight. I can't sleep. My body is sated but my mind prowls the past like it did while I lay as an invalid after Daphne's father tried to destroy me.

Was there something different I could have done to pry Daphne from her family? Is there any way we can have a future? My memories are a labyrinth, and I am lost. I'd wander forever, if it weren't for Daphne.

Daphne.

I sense her presence in the hall. Somehow—maybe her scent, or maybe I'm an animal, a predator, a hunter always aware of my surroundings. Or maybe we're attuned to one another. As much as I try to fight our connection, it's there.

A small knock and the door creaks open a sliver.

"Enter," I call.

She slips inside, a nymph in the moonlight. Her bare feet are silent as she approaches. She shivers slightly and I gesture for her to stand in front of the fire. Her piercings wink at me. Her eyes are hooded and tired.

I can't bring myself to order her around any more tonight. It was hard enough to leave her earlier tonight. I can't push her away a second time. I open my arms, letting my robe flop open. She crawls onto my bare chest, curling against me like the kitten I'm always calling her.

"I missed you," she murmurs against my neck. It feels so right, like always, having her here. Body against my body. Nuzzled against me, relaxed and trusting.

"I'm right here," I breathe out.

"No. You're far away." Her small fingers trace my mask, and for a second, I let her. Then I capture her hand, kiss her fingers and engulf them with mine.

She sighs long and loud. So much air for such a little body. I nuzzle her wet hair and study her profile as she stares at the fire. I want to believe her, to believe *this*, doesn't she understand?

But a man can only be broken so many times before there's nothing left to put back together.

"I thought it would be like this," she says, almost too low for me to hear.

"What?"

"Coming back. I thought we'd be together. And you'd be hurt and punish me, but mostly, it'd be like this." She nods to the fireplace.

"You and me cuddling in front of a fire?"

The firelight catches the side of her frown as she turns to me. "You and me, together."

I tuck a half-dry strand of hair behind her ear. "We are together."

"No we're not. You're holding yourself back, Logan."

My voice hardens, my body tensing. "Well, do you blame me?"

"No," she says, and looks sad. "I don't."

I rub soothing circles onto her back. "We still have this. Just for tonight." I can pretend for one night.

"Mmm," she hums, but it's not quite an agreement. She wants more than one night.

I wish I could give it to her.

"I called my dad today."

I bite back a grimace. Once upon a time, Dr. Laurel was my mentor. A surrogate father. I would have done anything to please him until I realized how hollow he was inside. Daphne's still caught in his web of lies.

"And?" I keep my voice bland.

She sighs. "He's still recovering. I talked to him today and he sounded so weak. I wanted to confront him about everything, challenge him about selling Thornhill but—"

"But?"

"In the end, does it matter? He's an old man. I've lived my whole life the way he wanted, but it was my choice. Especially the past few years, taking on Belladonna. I could've told him no."

My brows arch up. Daphne's never talked like this before. "Did you tell him that? Today?"

"No." She half rolls her eyes. "I kept our talk super short. He was slow and out of breath and I...well, I had a butt plug stretching my ass."

I can't help my chuckle. "You're such a good girl."

She giggles with me. "I so am."

Being with her feel so good, so natural. And since we're already pretending...

"Come. I have something to show you."

She lifts her head. "What?"

"A gift."

She sighs. "I only want you."

My cock jumps. Definitely *only* my cock. Not that other stupid organ in my chest. Not at all. I lift her off my lap, stand and offer my hand.

"An olive branch, then."

Daphne

"WON'T I NEED CLOTHES?" I ask as Logan wraps me in a fur carefully. "Shoes?"

"No. I'll carry you."

He lifts me as if I'm light as a rose petal. The night air is bracing on my bare face, but the coat covers me past my feet. Frosted grass crunches under Logan's shoes as he carries me down the hill. The castle looms behind us, darkly beautiful bathed in moonlight. Beside us, the labyrinth is a black, leafy wall.

But that's not where Logan is taking me. Moonlight glints off a structure ahead. I'm not wearing my contacts or glasses so it takes me a moment to recognize the sheen of glass.

"A greenhouse," I breathe, delighted.

When he opens the door, warm air embraces me, along with the scent of jasmine and vanilla. Logan sets me down. The moonlight is enough to guide my path through the dark rows. I can pick out the groups of plant by scent. Herbs, orchids, a few vegetables, and finally the last rows dedicated to hybrid after hybrid of—

"Roses." I swallow a stone that's suddenly formed in my throat. "These are my mother's."

I look to Logan and he doesn't deny it.

My eyes go back to the roses. "You brought them from Thornhill." I delicately touch a prickly leaf.

"I wanted them close," he says. "Easier to care for."

"My father told me he wouldn't let my mother's garden go, that he'd hire someone to keep it up. That the hybrids she was working on would be looked after, kept alive until I had time to return and continue her work." But he didn't. He sold Thornhill. It was Logan who cherished these roses and kept them thriving.

"Dad lied to me. About this. About everything." I turn and walk down the rows. Logan follows, a giant shadow dogging my steps. But I'm grateful for his presence. His warmth.

"Thornhill was promised to me, did you know that? I wanted to live there, convert one of the greenhouses to a lab. Dad convinced me to move into the city. Now I know why." I let out a hollow laugh.

I stop at the edge of the greenhouse and press my face to the cold glass. I won't cry. The hurt is so constant, it's seeped into my bones. It's part of my blood.

My father has always been like this. Since the day I was born, he made it clear that I mattered less than the stem cells I could give my ailing mother and the accolades I would win in his name. I've carried that pain and rejection every day of my life. Take it away and I wouldn't be Daphne.

LOGAN

THE PAIN in Daphne's voice stabs me. A tear beads in her lashes and she blinks it away.

"My father only cared about what I could give him. Never about me. I never mattered to him."

Finally, she sees the truth about her shit dad. There's no satisfaction in the fact, though, because I can see how much she's hurting. I reach out to touch her, but stop with my hand hovering in the air. I don't want to add to her pain.

Then she turns and sees my hand, smiles, and reaches up to clasp it herself. "I did matter to my mother. But I was her donor, you know. She loved me, she did, but our time together was colored by the disease. I never met anyone who cared about me for me...until I met you."

She looks up at me and I almost back away from her adoring smile. Her trust hits me like a blow.

"Everything's changing," she murmurs. "I'm changing. But I didn't do it fast enough, did I? As soon as I walked back into Belladonna, I turned into the old Daphne. A pushover, pleasing everyone but herself."

I start to make a noise and she goes on tiptoe to press two fingers to my lips.

"I'm not making excuses," she says quickly. "Everything that happened, I allowed it. But please, let me say this. I never got to properly say it when you found me that day at Mom's grave. I'm sorry. I'm so sorry for hurting you."

I swallow hard at her apology, not sure how I feel, but she's not done.

"Adam steamrolled over me and I let him. I was a grown

woman but I let him and fear of the board make me a doormat just like I always was for my father my whole life. And that's my fault."

She releases me and turns away.

"Anyway, I just wanted to finally say it out loud. I'm sorry I immediately fell back in old patterns. But the old mold doesn't fit anymore. In a way, it never did. I feel stronger now. I didn't know the world could be this...*big*. That my life could be so full of color. I feel like I'm starting to become the woman I was always supposed to be." Her voice grows stronger as she moves through the greenhouse. I catch up to her at the door. Her head's tipped back and the moonlight bathes her face. "And that's all because of you." The last words come out as a whisper but I hear them all the same.

"Come on," I wrap my arms around her. I can't help her words affecting me. She's saying everything I want to hear. And though there's a part of me that still clenched in suspicion of her playing me...the rest of me?

The rest of me just wants to hold my Daphne. Hold her close forever and never let her go.

"It's late. You need sleep for tomorrow."

"More torture?" she asks lightly.

I want to say no, but I can't lie. Owning Daphne's body is the only way to exorcise my demons. And if there's a chance, even the slightest chance that this could all be real, that there could be a future for us...

"It's okay," she whispers, and snuggles against me as I carry her to bed. I tuck her in, careful of her piercings. I fuss as long as I can until there's nothing left to do. But I can't bring myself to leave. I slide my hand over the coverlet, smoothing it over and over again, feeling her warmth underneath.

"Lie with me?" she asks sleepily. She's so beautiful, soft and warm in the bed, inviting and tempting like nothing else. It's a bad idea, but I can't refuse. I'm tired of fighting. There's nothing else I want than to hold her close for hours.

"This isn't a precedent," I mutter as I slip in next to her. Her smooth legs tangle with mine and my boner tents the sheet. I grit my teeth, willing it to subside. I really do just want to hold her and I'm not sure I could deal with the intensity of fucking her again right now. If I started, I'm not sure I could stop. "I'm not doing this every night," I growl churlishly.

She doesn't acknowledge my warning. "You were the only one who could get me to sleep," she reminds me, sighing happily and tucking her head under my chin. Her breathing evens out immediately, leaving me wondering if I'm living my nightmare or my best dream.

TWENTY

Present Day
Daphne

The sun slants across my face and I stretch. Logan is gone—I didn't expect he'd stay. That he held me last night so I could fall sleep is enough.

Last night felt...important. Like maybe a breakthrough of some kind? Even if only for me. It was important for me to officially apologize and acknowledge my responsibility for what happened. I can't control what Logan believes. I can only control my actions and responses.

And I'm done being a doormat. For my father. For Logan. For anyone.

He left long instructions for my day. No more butt plugs, thank gods. My ass still feels stretched and sore—in the most delicious way.

I take his list of commands and head to the bathroom. Submitting sexually to Logan is different than being a doormat. I'm participating *with* him and there's a willing exchange of control. It's thrilling and life-giving.

When I look in the mirror, a beautiful, vibrant woman looks back, her eyes wide and soft and filled with satisfaction. No longer a mousy wallflower who thinks she should stay quiet in the background.

I arch my back and examine myself. My nipple piercings look good. The area is still a bit red, but no sign of infection. I perform the aftercare per Logan's instructions and soak my breasts in a sea salt solution. Logan also left a can of saline wash with orders to mist my nipples several times a day. If I don't, he says he'll punish me and oversee the aftercare himself.

The threats make me smile. If he has his way, the piercings will heal perfectly, and I'll always remember last night, his claim. He's making sure he's always a part of me.

Even if I take out the piercings, he'll always be a part of me. Permanently. But then, he would have been without the piercings, anyway.

As I return to the bedroom, my phone chirps from the drawer I tossed it in. I've been ignoring it—sending Rachel the bare minimum of texts to keep her from calling the cops. Should I take a picture of my nipples and send it to her? I grin at the thought.

The phone screen tells me she's called three times already this morning. I quickly sober. She's probably not in the mood to hear about my sex life.

Time to face reality. I click the call button and wander to a seat by the fire. I'm naked but for a towel around my waist. Logan's trained me to feel comfortable in the buff. Yet another thing for Rachel and I to giggle about during our next girl's night.

Rachel picks up on the second ring. "Oh thank gods,"

she gasps. "I have good news, and I have bad news."

I rub my forehead. "Go ahead."

"The good news is...Adam hasn't bothered you these past few days."

She's right. He's been quiet. Not a call, not even a text.

"What's the bad news?"

"Well...the reason he's not bothering you is he's busy planning your engagement party."

I almost drop the phone. "What?!" I start to pace. "Shit, Rachel, that is bad news."

"Um, that's not the bad news. I kinda might have promised him you'd be there. You know, at your own engagement party."

I groan and collapse into a chair. A hoard of workmen have moved into my head, and they must be doing demolition, because my head is pounding.

"I know," Rachel whispers. "I couldn't stop him. I could only buy time. He's left you alone because he thinks you're resting up and getting ready for the ball."

"A ball? You mean the engagement party?"

"He kinda invited everyone in Olympus. At least, everyone who matters."

Meaning: the rich and famous and powerful. The jackhammering in my skull increases.

"The board?"

"Yep."

"The donors?"

"Unfortunately."

"Fuck."

"Yeah," Rachel agrees. "I couldn't stop him. When I wouldn't give him your location, he was going to track your cellphone and show up to surprise you."

I clutch the phone. I am having a heart attack. There's

no other way to describe this tightness in my chest.

"Daphne?"

Breathe, just breathe.

"Okay, Rachel. Thank you. When is the ball?"

"Tomorrow."

"Of course it is." I can't react with shock—I have no more to give. "Can you get a dress and stylist ready?"

"You're going?"

"Of course I am." What better time to break off my engagement? Not ideal, but it has to be done.

It's time to finally stand up to Adam.

Ten minutes later I knock on the library door. I'm dressed in jeans and a t-shirt, a brand new sports bra cradling my breasts. Feels weird to be wearing clothes.

Logan's reading a paper, ignoring my approach. I almost go to my knees, but decide against it. We need to have this conversation as equals.

"Logan, I need to talk to you about something."

He lowers the paper and blinks at my clothed form. His ice-blue gaze pierces me. His mask is white today. "I think you mean, 'Master.'"

But I don't lower my head. "Yes, you're Master, but you're also more than that. You're Logan and I'm Daphne. And I need to be able to talk to you."

I walk forward to the table and climb onto his lap. His jaw flexes and his hands come to my hips. For a second, I'm not sure if he wants to toss me off or not, but then his hands start to massage my flesh. Oh, his touch feels *so* good. I want to melt into him and languish in his touch. I want to go back to last night when he held me in his arms and it felt like he was beginning to trust me.

But no, I have to stay strong. This has to be said.

So I hurry to get it out all at once. "Adam's planning an

engagement party. I just found out. It's tomorrow."

Logan's frozen to stone underneath me. And his voice is ice when he asks, "Are you looking for my permission?"

"What? Gods, no! I'm telling you I need to go break it off with him. To his face. It all got out of hand. I never said yes—"

"Then how did his ring get on your finger?"

Logan hoists me by my waist and deposits me on the floor. Apparently he can't stand my touch or proximity anymore because he prowls to the far side of the room.

"No. I forbid it. If you want your father's patents, you aren't to leave the grounds."

He's lashing out like a wounded animal.

I approach Logan with my head held high. "I was weak then but I'm strong enough now. I know I am." All I can do is reiterate what I said last night and pray that he's strong too. Strong enough to believe in me. In us. "You've shown me my own strength. You've let me explore who I am and who I want to be. I know my mind and what I want."

I reach out a hand to touch his cheek. "And it was never Adam."

He still flinches when I say Adam's name.

"I don't trust him," he growls, his eyes narrowing behind his mask.

"Do you trust me?" I ask.

His jaw tightens again and I see the conflict in his eyes as he finally says, "I'm trying to."

Oh, Logan. What happened to this man that's made it so hard for him to trust? But he's trying. He just said so and I've seen it firsthand. It means so, so much. It means that there's a chance for us.

So I kneel on the floor at his feet and bow my head. And utter one simple word. "Master."

TWENTY-ONE

Present Day
Logan

She's so beautiful and perfectly submissive. Or is it all an act? The constant question that tortures me.

Her request has taken me off guard.

But she came to you. She didn't try to hide or run off behind your back. And she wants to break the engagement. And the reality is, last night things shifted. I swore I saw the truth shining in her eyes. Can I trust it? Can I trust my own judgment when it comes to her?

At some point, there has to be a leap of faith. She's sure as hell asking me to leap, wanting to go to this fucking engagement party. But what she said, about being strong now... Will I be weak when she's strong?

She's continually abandoned herself to me and put herself in my hands, so bravely.

I'll show her that I can be brave too, and I'll send her out into the world stronger than she's ever been.

I'll fucking leap.

And all the while, there she kneels, so gorgeous, her fall of black hair so silky and smooth, at my feet.

"Strip," I order. "And follow me."

She immediately pulls her shirt off her head and discards her bra, then shimmies out of her leggings and underwear, exposing acres of golden skin.

My erection immediately pulses to life. I want to grab her and mount her right here. But that's too exposed and besides, with as unsteady as I feel, I know a scene will do us both good.

I lead her to the dungeon. The one place where things have always made sense between us. My thudding heartbeat calms as soon as we step into the room. Yes. Calm. Control. It soothes over me like the ocean tide.

Daphne is silent, observing, peeking up even though her head is lowered. Naughty sub.

"Eyes down." I give her ass a swat.

She lowers her eyes and twitches in place, rubbing her legs together. I grow even harder. She's as excited for this as I am. Maybe she knows she needs it, too. She said I make her stronger, and she's going to need that strength if she's going to go back out in the world to face everyone who cowed her before.

I put my hand on the small of her back and lead her over to the spanking bench.

It's a custom piece, leather-bound with padded knee-stands and arm rests, along with an amply stuffed chest piece for her to lay face down on without disturbing her nipple piercings.

She climbs on with no inhibitions. So damn brave. I help place her limbs in the correct position. Her pussy is exposed so beautifully and I can already see that she's wet. She responds so well to her Master.

The rush of adrenaline hits me all at once and we've barely even started. I want to ride this high forever.

"Don't move," I order, then quickly, I walk to a nearby cabinet and gather supplies. I'm back only moments later, running a smooth length of rope between my fingers.

"Keep still," I whisper again as I begin to bind her wrists, looping the rope down to her elbows and capturing her in place like a beautiful butterfly pinned to a board, first one arm and then another. I want her to feel the constraint like an embrace, holding her still, folding her in. Keeping her safe.

Then I move to her ankles and repeat the same process there, winding the rope up her calves and binding her in place. Her toes flex in response and I smooth a hand down her skin after I'm done.

"Good girl."

The bindings have spread her legs even wider, her pussy perfectly exposed. Along with that gorgeous ass of hers.

I can't help running a hand down her spine and then grabbing both globes in a harsh, massaging grip. She squirms underneath me and uses the smallest, limited bit of movement she has to lift her hips and push more into my grasp.

Her enthusiasm for my touch and our play—gods, it gets me every time. I squeeze harder, digging my thumbs in as I massage her flesh.

But no, I can't let myself get distracted.

I have a plan. And new toys.

I pull away from her and walk over to the newest toy. I have to wheel it over. She tries to look over her shoulder to see what I'm doing, but I prepared. The bench is angled so that she's got no view.

"I've got a surprise in store for you, pet."

I prepared it earlier today and I wheel it right up to her opening. I didn't get the height quite right and I have to make some adjustments. But with just a few turns of the lever, the contraption with the large dildo on a retractable pump is ready to go.

I start slow and add a little lube to the huge, flesh colored vibrator.

I don't turn it on at first, just wheel it even closer so that she can feel the large silicon cock at the lips of her sex.

I've moved over to her side so I can see the look on her face. One of the highest thrills of being a Dom is watching every reaction on her face to each new sensation I introduce.

She's surprised and, I note, a little disappointed.

"I wish it was you," she whispers. Her words make my chest tighten in pleasure, but still I lean over and whisper right in her ear, "You have to earn Master's cock in your pussy."

And fuck me, but I enjoy the shiver that runs down her spine and the goosebumps that rise all over her pretty flesh.

More rise when I continue, "But right now you're going to be fucked the way Master wants. And you're going to love every minute of what I do to your body."

She nods even as a large, explosive breath puffs out of her chest.

"Now relax, kitten, and take what Master gives you."

I run my hands down both of her hips and then nudge the contraption closer, penetrating her pussy.

She gasps as she opens to it.

It's large. Larger than almost any man. It's stretching her.

I keep an eye on her face, hungry to experience every new moment of sensation with her. Where I'm taking her, I want to participate in every moment of the journey.

I bite my lip even as my cock fights at the seam of my pants.

"That's right, kitten. Now we're going to start moving."

She hiccups a breath but then nods.

I keep one hand on her hip as I turn the machine on to its lowest setting, both vibration wise and pistoning in and out.

But no matter how prepared she thought she was, nothing could have equipped her for the machine and the monster cock attached to it.

Her hands grip desperately at the leather of the bench and her toes curl as the vibrator begins to slowly invade her, in and out. It comes out covered in her juices, slick and glistening.

"It's stretching you so wide, isn't it?" I breathe out. "You can barely stand it. But you'll do it for Master, won't you?"

She nods, looking up to where I stand. "Yes. For you."

"You can take it. I'll never give you more than you can take. You know that."

She nods, and tears glisten in her eyes. But they aren't tears of pain. Her body has relaxed, her grip loosened. "I trust you," she whispers and her eyes flutter closed.

She's giving herself over to it.

Truly submitting.

Trusting me completely.

And the flood of power and security and control at her

trusting me to take her there, at being with her in this moment—

I want more.

I want it all.

I remove the mask I've been wearing and set it aside. Daphne's eyes widen when I stalk around the bench, viewing her from every angle. I'm not going to take it easy on her. That's not what she needs right now.

"Beg me for more."

A line creases her forehead even as she starts to squirm on the bench. I know the expression well. She's chasing her pleasure and wants to please me. Gods, the rush—

More. I need more than just watching. I need contact. I need to be more intimately connected. Now. Because I need this as much as she does.

I pour lube on my finger and then I approach her backside. I know where I want to go. I need her to open herself completely.

This willingness to trust her is so new and if I'm honest, there are still doubts... But if I can strip her bare, take her to her deepest, most vulnerable place and connect with her there, then maybe I'll finally know the truth for certain.

"Open for me," I command. "Don't hold anything back."

I slide my finger down her ass and approach her dark little rosette. I don't wait or give her time to brace. That's the whole point. No hiding.

I tease my finger around her anal entrance and then press inside.

Her muscles are loose. Maybe from last night, or maybe because it's impossible to clench while she's being plowed by the machine.

That doesn't mean she doesn't notice the intrusion. She

cries out and her entire body shudders. She feels everything, might even be more hypersensitive.

And I love it. I love every second of feeling her hot, tight body coiled around my finger. I love feeling the jolt as the vibrator bottoms out inside her and pulls back, and her little *oofs* and moans of surprise and pleasure.

I'm opening her up in every way.

I press another finger in and finally, I meet some resistance. She's taken me before, but not with a cock in her pussy at the same time.

"I don't know if I can," she whines.

"You can and you will."

"But—"

"I am your Master and you trust me. Now give your body over to me. Give yourself to me completely."

I crank the machine a notch higher and it begins fucking her faster. She jolts with every thrust in and I continue my exploration of her ass.

I don't intend for this to go quickly. I want her body worn out. At its limits.

So I continue to explore her ass to my heart's content, delighting in the contours of her body and feeling her every reaction from the inside as she gives in.

She gives in, but never stops reacting. It's part of what makes her so special. She never takes a moment for granted. She continues to *feel* everything.

She's impossible and refuses subspace almost willfully, like she's so desperate to hold onto every second of feeling and sensation.

But I'll take her there. I'm determined to give her that gift. To take her so far inside her body that she's able to float out of it.

I withdraw my fingers and quickly wash my hands at a

sink in the corner, then return and pick up a soft leather flogger.

"You trust me, so give yourself over to me." I run the flogger over her ass and then flick it, smacking her bottom with the tresses.

I continue in a rotating infinity pattern, raining down smacks in a pattern that has her ass quickly turning a beautiful pink.

Every couple of minutes, I pause and check her face. I've been keeping it light. At this point, I just want the buildup of a slow intensity.

But I think I'm getting where I want to go, because her moans have been getting lower and deeper and her eyes have dropped to half-mast. We've been at it for about twenty-five minutes.

Her inhibitions are down. She's giving in. It's an almost unconscious process, but for it to work, it requires absolute trust.

I want to prolong it. I'm not nearly ready to let this go, I feel like a fucking conqueror with her so limp and compliant and riding high beneath me, her body a ship I'm carefully captaining.

It's time to relax for a little now, to prepare for what will eventually come. I massage her ass, rubbing in the sting while not creating any more. Again her moans deepen. I want to record the sound to play back on repeat.

I'm hard as stone but it's not important right now. I have a job to do and I mean to do it perfectly.

For the next ten minutes, I keep her at altitude by applying a heavier smack with the flogger every minute or so and then continuing with my massage. In truth, I'm as desperate for the contact with her flushed skin as I'm hoping she is. If her satisfied moans are anything to go by, she's loving every single thing happening to her.

When I check her face next, she looks even further gone and I know it's time. Higher impact, another intense five-minute push. I switch out the flogger for a cane and start to stripe her ass, up and down.

She jerks and groans with every strike, her body trembling and pussy suctioning and slurping and making fucking pornographic noises around the vibrator as it thrusts in and out of her.

At the end of the five minutes I toss the cane away and pick up the small pocket vibrator, switching it on and moving to her side. I reach underneath her hip, around to her clit.

She jolts and cries out in ecstasy the moment I make contact. I bend over her body and hold onto her ass, one finger curving towards her hole. I want to touch every inch of her possible.

"Break for me," I whisper, pressing my forehead to her ear. "Break for me and give me everything."

She howls and shudders as her orgasm breaks, tears streaming down her cheeks in huge rivulets.

"That's right," I murmur, bending even closer. "Yes, that's so good. Don't hold back. Give me it all." The whole time I keep mercilessly at her clit and she howls from the bottom of her lungs.

She's magnificent. I've never in my life seen or even experienced such a pure exaltation of pleasure and abandon. But I experience it through her. *With* her.

I don't know how long it goes on but it feels like forever, and at the same time, over far too soon.

But when she's limp and laying crumpled over the bench, I know she's had enough. I hurry to turn off the machine and slowly, gently disengage it from her drenched, dripping pussy and roll it backwards.

I'll come back for cleanup and sterilization later.

Right now she's the most important thing.

Swiftly I untie the soft shibari ropes and free her. She continues lying limp against the bench even though I've released her.

Holy shit, I really took her there, didn't I?

And I know what comes after is every bit as important. Gods, she's gorgeous when she's like this. As magnificent as she was howling in the heights of her pleasure, subdued and limp in the aftermath, she glows with a purity that stabs me through the chest.

This is Daphne. My Daphne.

The woman who knocked me off my ass the first time she came strutting down the beach in a red bikini. The woman who laughed with me and teased me and splashed in the water with me all one glorious summer. The woman I held in my arms after her mother died and her world fell apart.

This is Daphne.

The woman I—

The woman I *love*.

Terror chokes me even as I gather her into my arms like the precious thing she is. She curls into me and her fingers brush my bare face, her touch making me harden all over again. The softest butterfly brush and then her hand drops as if she's too tired to hold it up.

What is she doing to me?

She could destroy me. She's proved it. Over and over and maybe I'm a fool for never learning.

Or maybe I'm finally opening myself to the best thing of my life.

Me and Daphne, finally together. Like we were always meant to be.

My chest feels so incredibly warm as I carry Daphne upstairs to take care of her, wash her, and tuck her in close by my side for the night.

I never want to let her go.

TWENTY-TWO

Present Day
Daphne

There's a warm wall at my back—huge and unyielding as a mountain. I roll and gently collide with a muscular chest dusted with dark hair. The mountain stirs. I throw an arm around him, hugging him close.

"Careful." Logan eases me back, frowning at my nipples.

"You stayed." Happiness rolls over me, a warm blanket. It feels like a dream.

"You need sleep," he says gruffly. "If you get sick, your piercings can get infected."

I'm smiling so hard my skin might crack. The corner of Logan's mouth hitches up in response to my giddiness. *He stayed. He cares.*

The fire is out and the room is chilly. Logan bundles me up carefully in a blanket and carries me to the bathroom where he performs the piercing aftercare himself. He washes the rest of me so thoroughly, my knees wobble, weak with arousal.

I'm panting by the time he's done, hoping he'll bend me over the tub and fuck me. But no. He leads me out and dries me off, then steps back into the shower and soaps up his massive body while I watch. Rivulets run in the grooves between his insane muscles. His hands are huge as they swipe soap over his delectable abs.

I lick my lips. I'm staring. I can't help it. When he lathers up his palms to wash his cock, my pussy pulses with a mini-orgasm. He shoots me a wicked look.

I take a step towards him and he shakes his head. "Stay."

He turns his back to me to wash his hair under the spray and the eyeful I get of his chiseled back and ass makes me drop to my knees. I'd crawl to him right now and beg for him to let me take him in my mouth. I'd grovel for a chance to touch him, kiss his feet.

He could have reacted so differently when I made my request yesterday. But he was gracious, kind, the perfect Master playing my body like a prodigy and taking me further than I'd ever been— so deep, so high, so excruciatingly *intimate* together with him, and that's not even to speak of the pleasure—

I want to worship him back. I've never wanted anything more. And he knows it. When he exits the shower and slings a towel around his hips, I groan.

"Such a needy little one," he murmurs, nothing but affection in his tone.

I look up from my knees in pure reverence.

He bends down and lifts me, setting me on a towel spread on the marble vanity top. Then *he* kneels.

"What are you doing?" I ask as he bends his dark, wet head and kisses the inside of my thigh just above my knee.

"Something to remember me by," he rasps, easing my legs open. And then....oh...his mouth... He licks me all over, adding scratchy kisses courtesy of his unshaven face. There's no mask between us.

It feels like years since I've seen his beloved face. The scarred portion on his left cheek is just a feature of his face to me now. All I see is Logan. My Logan, more dear to me than anyone else on this earth.

I cum as our gazes lock, my head flying back and hitting the bathroom mirror almost hard enough to crack it. Logan picks me up and brings me to a chair in front of the fire. He bustles around, dressing and building up the fire while I sit, still floating.

An alarm goes off somewhere in the room. Distantly I hear it, but don't recall what it is. Not until Logan lays my phone down next to me. I set an alarm earlier, reminding me to pack. For my engagement ball.

"You need to go," Logan says.

I open my mouth to protest, and I realize he's not kicking me out. He's letting me go...again. To deal with Adam.

Logan kneels again in front of me. In his palm is a ring. My heart flutters a second in blinding joy, and then I realize it's the gaudy diamond Adam picked out for me. My throat squeezes. I don't want to touch it.

But Logan plucks it and pinches it between thumb and forefinger, holding it in front of my face. "I know you need to go back."

I swallow and nod. Logan sets my phone and the ring on a side table.

"You'll return to me," he says. His finger traces a wide circle around my pierced nipples. "You'll remember me."

"Yes." I cup his face. "I can do this, Logan. You can trust me."

An hour later, a familiar car pulls up. I'm dressed warmly. My nipple piercings are carefully bound, but they chafe. A constant reminder of the one I'm leaving. The one I belong to.

He's trusting me. I won't fail him. Not this time.

TWENTY-THREE

Present Day
Daphne

In the car I grab my phone and dial my dad. The call doesn't connect until we're out of the hills and forest and on the road to New Olympus. But then it rings and rings for a while until a nurse picks up.

"Is my father all right?" I ask after we exchange greetings.

The nurse hesitates. "He's sleeping now. I'd wake him but--"

"Oh, no, it's fine. He needs his sleep." He's been sleeping more and more lately. I give instructions for the nurse to call me when he wakes. I'm sure Adam pestered him about coming to the engagement party. I add that to my list of things to confront my 'fiancé' about.

Can't wait. Not. If I could, I'd tell the driver to turn the car around.

But no. The new Daphne doesn't avoid conflict. Still, all too soon the car is pulling up to one of the first high rises built in New Olympus, a grand old building repurposed into an event space. I order the driver to pull around back to avoid the caterers and crew setting up in the ballroom downstairs. Hopefully I can get my dress, hair, and makeup done before anyone sees me.

Rachel is pacing in a fancy private parlor on the second floor. "Daphne," she breathes and I rush to give her a hug. Wow, I've really missed her. So much has happened. I could use a friend to confide in.

"You okay?" she draws back to study my face. She looks worried but I just give her arm a squeeze.

"Yep. Let's do this." I strip quickly out of my clothes.

"Holy shit. You're pierced." Rachel's mouth hangs open.

Oops. "Yes." No use feigning a shyness I don't feel. I'm not ashamed. I go to the mirror to inspect the piercings.

"When?"

"Logan did it."

Rachel shakes her head, but says nothing as I pull my saline spray from my purse. I ignore her, sharing a shy smile with the woman in the mirror.

Thank you, Logan, for marking me. Just seeing them reminds me of who I am. Of my strength. Warmth pools in my lower belly as I care for my piercings as he ordered.

"Um, I got a few dresses, but with those," Rachel waves at my chest, "This one might be the best option." She holds up a gold dress with a sweetheart top.

"No," I say. "I ordered something myself. It should've been delivered with the rest." At Rachel's skeptical look, I smile and add, "No tree costume this time, I promise." I go to the roller rack of dresses and rummage until I find the green sheath. "Here." Green reminds me of Logan, and I need all the reminders I can get.

Rachel pauses as I hold up the dress against myself, eyeing me.

"What?"

"Nothing," she says, but then she crosses her arms over her chest. "There's something different about you." She rolls her eyes. "Apart from the obvious." She gestures at my boobs but then gets serious again, obviously waiting for my answer.

There are a thousand things on the tip of my tongue. I want to tell her about all of it. About Logan and how amazing and electric he is. About the future I've only begun daring to hope for with him. About how screwed up everything is with the company and Adam, complicated even more by how much Logan hates him and—

I reach out and grab Rachel's hand. "Let's just get through tonight. This week, you and me. We'll go out for coffee or stay in and have a movie night and download everything going on in each other's lives."

Rachel squeezes my hand back. "I'll hold you to that promise. Now, get your ass in this chair so the stylist can do her wonders. She'll be here any sec—" Right then the doorbell rings and Rachel springs up to go answer it.

An hour later, my hair and make up are done and I'm in the sheath dress. The neckline is high enough to keep my nipples in a full coverage bra. Rachel pleads and I change into red lingerie she brought, tags still on. The bra is simple but the thong is lace. She looks so relieved, I have a thought.

"Why do you want me to wear this so badly? Did you buy it?"

She hesitates, obviously torn.

"Wait, Adam bought me this, didn't he?" Part of me

wants to take it off and put back on my own on principle, but my cotton briefs show a panty line. And besides, it's not like Adam's ever going to see me in the lingerie set.

"It's okay," I wave a hand. "Zip me up?" I bow my head and Rachel obliges.

"I'm sorry, Daphne," Rachel says softly. "Adam's been insistent on certain things. I know you're my boss but…"

"But one day he might be too." Guilt flushes me. I've been thinking of myself, considering my options, but I'm not the only one affected by the Belladonna merger. And Rachel isn't just my friend. She's my employee. "It's fine. I put you in a tough position, and I want you to know that I appreciate having you in my corner."

She gives me a thin smile. There are lines on her forehead and around her eyes that I've never noticed before. This whole ordeal has weighed on her.

"Hey, I know," I say on impulse. "After all this is done, let's just get away together. You and me. Not just for coffee. We'll have a girl's spa weekend. The full pampering treatment."

"Okay," Rachel says, but she doesn't look at me. "I've got to go change."

"Of course." I drop her hand and head to the mirror to check out my 'do. The stylist worked wonders, but there's a flush to my cheeks that's more than makeup. I'm glowing.

"So how's tonight going to go?" Rachel asks from behind the screen where she's changing into her own gown. "What are you going to say to Adam?"

"What I should've said in the first place." I raise my chin at the woman in the mirror. She looks strong, determined. *Game time.* "I'm going to break off the engagement."

Rachel is silent until she emerges. She's wearing a sheath in a floral pattern.

"Oh you look so great," I gush but she doesn't smile. Her face is pale.

"How? The board and everyone will be here."

"I'll be discreet. I don't want to cause a scene." I shrug. I haven't let myself sweat the details. It's enough that I'm here and that I'm not leaving without this engagement being broken. "I'll pull Adam aside and tell him. Honestly, he's the one who planned this party. I'd have told him no, if he'd consulted me."

Rachel looks so suddenly panicked, I catch her hand again. It's cold as marble.

"Sheesh, you're freezing," I chafe her hand. "You look a bit pale. Are you feeling okay?"

"Fine. I just haven't eaten all day." She draws up her cheeks in a forced smile but there's still worry in her eyes. "Come on," she says. "Adam and the guests are waiting."

I HAVE TO CREDIT ADAM; he has great taste in everything but engagement rings. And he knows how to throw a party. The building is gorgeous. The foyer is dripping with floral displays. I stop on the grand marble staircase and take in the sea of about a thousand roses. One display is smaller but more tasteful. I recognize the blowsy blooms as pink Edens, a climbing variety of garden rose.

Rachel pauses beside me. "Your father sent those."

Shit. Dad. I never called back to try to catch him after his nap. "He's not coming? He's been resting a lot when I call but the nurse said he's been feeling better lately."

"Adam told him about the engagement party," Rachel says. "Dr. Laurel was pleased."

Of course he was. Dad always did like things neat and

tidy. "I need to call him." Tell him I'm breaking my engagement to his favorite surrogate son. Dad will be disappointed. A pang goes through me at the thought, but I shake my head.

What does it matter what my dad thinks? It's my life. I get to choose who to marry and I deserve to be happy. Why does that feel like such a rebellious thought? It's absurd that choosing my own happiness should have to feel like such an act of courage. But it only makes me more determined to stand firm in my new truth.

As Rachel leads me down a side hall so we can slip into the back of the ballroom, an image of me marrying Logan, dressed in a slave collar, jeweled piercings and nothing else flies through my head. I grin at the ridiculous thought, but then sigh. Dad would have a fit if I even mentioned the name 'Logan' and 'marry' in the same sentence. Better break it to him gently.

Then my eyes fly open wide at the thoughts so casually running through my head. Not that Logan wants to *marry* me. It's too soon to be thinking about that. Ridiculous. Completely ridiculous. I need to sort out my life first and he's never even said—

"Here we are," Rachel says, breaking into my thoughts as she pauses before a back door to the ballroom. Beyond the white and gilt doors, the crowd murmuring is a dull roar.

"One sec." I check my purse and pull out my phone. No missed calls. Nothing from dad. Or Logan. Am I happy or sad about the latter? "The nurse said she'd have Dad call when he woke up. She must have forgotten--"

"Shit, Daphne," Rachel interrupts. "do you have the ring?"

Right. Almost forgot. I pull it out of my purse. "Right here."

A bevy of servers, dressed in black tuxedos with gold cummerbunds, stream by. Rachel pulls me into an alcove.

"Are you going to wear it?" Rachel's eyes are wide.

"No." Rach looks so shocked, I take pity on her. "I have a plan." I dig in my purse and pull out the long green opera gloves I ordered along with the dress. I tug them on and drop the ring back in my purse, then waggle my fingers at Rachel. "See? Doesn't go with the outfit." She looks doubtful, but I pull out of a pair of white gloves for her. "It'll make sense when we match."

I check my phone again as she pulls on her own pair of gloves but no texts or calls have come in in the last minute and I put it away.

"Ready?" I ask.

"I guess. You seem eager."

"I am." I can't believe it, but I am. I'm ready to get this done with and prove to myself once and for all that I have changed. I place a hand on the fancy gilt door, ready to push it open. Nervousness flutters in my chest, but I expect it, embrace it.

For the first time in my life, I'm owning what I want. And I'm going to fight until I get it.

TWENTY-FOUR

7 Years Ago
Logan

I flip through the secure notes from the investor meeting while standing in the lab. I had to do some finagling to even get my hands on these but there are still some people in the company who know how closely I work with Dr. Laurel and respect me.

Ha. That's a joke if I ever heard one, but I'll take what I can get while I can get it. I haven't talked to the great Professor in weeks and I barely even caught a glimpse of him at the funeral. I was far more concerned with Daphne, whom the great Dr. Laurel barely took note of. His own daughter.

I used to think he was a great man doing great things.

Now I think he's just…lost. And he never treated his daughter right. But if he's not careful, his company is going to get stolen out from underneath him by his board, headed by that blond bastard, Adam Archer.

I flip to a third page and my eyes scan the first few lines. "What the fuck?"

I slap the papers down, disbelieving, before lifting them back up and continuing to read. "That son of a bitch." I knew Adam was a slimy opportunist, but I didn't realize he was *this* slimy.

Footsteps have me looking up, and there he is, the son of a bitch in question.

He's got a shiny apple in hand and he takes a big, obnoxious bite. "Miss me?" he asks through his mouthful of apple.

I point at him. "I see you. I see what you're trying to do to this company."

"What?" He throws his hands in the air. "Make it profitable? Bring out the firing squad for such a horrible offense."

Jackass. "I know what you did. I know you took credit for all my innovations in the lab. Anyone with eyes can check the lab logs and know it would've been impossible for you to have discovered what you said you did. You haven't even *been here*."

But he just laughs at me. "You think anyone gives a shit about *lab logs*? It's all about the package." He swipes up and down himself. "'Golden-boy-genius saves company' makes a far better story than 'some street rat diddles himself in lab for years, not in time to save the boss's wife but look, here's some face cream out of it at least'—"

I grab him by his shirt and slam him up against the nearest wall.

He just smirks at me and speaks in a condescending tone. "Yes, violence is always the answer to you low-class types, isn't it? Help me help you on your way out. Take a swing."

I drop him and take several stumbling steps back. This is all a game to him. A game where he thinks he's pulling the strings. He thinks he's always in control.

"Too bad. That was your last chance. Shoulda taken it."

I glare up at him, but not in time. I don't see him coming until he's almost on top of me, fists swinging.

"Fucker!" I shout, and try to get an arm up to block, but I'm too late. His blow lands square on my left cheek, and it knocks me to the floor. He's wearing a class ring and it digs in and tears my flesh, so there's blood running down my cheek when he's done.

He dances back to his feet and smooths down his suit coat and pants. Then he just shakes his head at me on the floor in disgust. "You're done here. Pack your shit and leave."

I want to get up, roar in rage, and tear his fucking face off. Anyone who really knows the guy would understand and cheer me on.

But that's the thing. Nobody *does* know the real Adam Archer. He's that plastic for a reason—so everyone believes the benign Ken-doll act. It's his secret weapon.

And what happens to Daphne if I suddenly go to jail for assault and battery. Because if I started in on Adam, I don't know if I could stop. Where does that leave the girl who's always left behind, last in everyone's considerations?

I can't be one more person she counts on to just up and disappear from her life.

Even thinking of her makes all the shit I'm feeling a little less oppressive. I pull my phone out of my lab coat and call her. I know it's old school, an actual phone call, but I'd kill to hear her voice right now.

She doesn't answer, but I still close my eyes and sink back against the wall while I listen to her message: *This is Daphne's phone. I'm not here right now but leave a message and...yada yada, you know the rest. Bye!*

It would be creepy to call back just so I can listen to her chipper voice on the message, right? And I know it was recorded a long time ago, back before her mom died. She's having a hard time with everything, not that you'd know it by the way she's absolutely disappeared into her studies.

Some kids would've abandoned working so hard after losing the parent all the work was intended to save, but not Daph. Never Daph. It was like there was a new fire under her butt now that Battleman's had taken her mom, like she wanted to say F you to the disease even more, and was more determined than ever to figure out what made it tick and how to stop it.

Like father, like daughter, except that I suspected if Daphne ever had children, she's take all the time in the world to love and cherish them.

For just a brief second, I let the fantasy take shape, Daphne and I coming home from the lab together, picking the kids up from school, then all going home to cook a rambunctious dinner...a family, a home, everything I never had but always dreamed of...or really only let myself dream of since meeting *her*.

Everything seems possible when I'm with her. It's her magic.

But she's still so young, and vulnerable after her mother's death. I can't go with all this to her—she's still in college, already working too hard and the last one I want Adam pointing his sights on is her if he decides she's a threat to his plan.

And that means I need to fight for her company. Because she can't yet.

Which leaves only one person left to put a stop to Adam's ambitions before he destroys us all.

I need to go have a chat with Dr. Laurel.

WHEN I KNOCK on the door to Daphne's father's office, at first I don't hear anything.

"I told you, he's asked for no visitors," his aged assistant chides.

"Well, he needs to speak to me or he's going to have his company stolen right out from under him."

She purses her lips but then sits back in her chair and picks up her yarn needles.

"Dr. Laurel," I pound on the door again, since her calling his office had no effect. "It's Logan. I need to speak to you."

Finally, *finally*, there's movement from within and the doorknob creaks open. He doesn't stay at the door to greet me, He just pulls it open and then disappears back into the dark room.

There are no lights on. The blinds aren't open. Maybe my eyes will adjust but after the bright fluorescents of the waiting room, it first appears pitch black in here. I can only *barely* make out the shape of a man sitting behind his desk, and it's only when he moves, to take a drink of something, that I'm sure.

I clear my throat. I'll just pretend like nothing's wrong. Probably the best way to play this. "Look, Sir, I don't know what the best way to tell you this is, but Adam Archer is trying to steal your company out from underneath you and turn it into something completely different than you ever envisioned."

I wait for him to say something, to sound aggrieved or apologetic or appalled by the situation, but I'm only met with silence.

"That is to say, sir, as you can see here," I pull the papers recounting the minutes of the board meeting and thrust them on the desk in front of his face, "Here Archer clearly states that the lab discoveries of the new molecule were made by *him*, with no mention of you or me. And he further proposed that a full 95% of Belladonna's resources be poured into cosmetics research and production instead of our core mission to cure pernicious diseases—"

Dr. Laurel suddenly stands up, so violently his chair shoves backward into the wall behind him. "What does any of it matter? She's gone, so who the fuck cares now?"

"But—" I sputter. "But you were the one who told me how much the *world* needed our research, how it was never just about one patient, it was—"

"Fuck the world!" He swipes a furious forearm and clears his desk of everything on it in one crashing swoop. "Without her there's nothing! *Nothing.*"

And then the paragon of strength and brilliance I'd looked up to for years dissolved into a puddle right in front of me, sobbing into his own armpit.

I want to turn away. Daphne deserves better than him. She always has. For him to just give up like this, in a room that smells sour with sweat and booze, while she's out there busting her tail, I know in part to prove herself to this man...

But I start to approach him anyway. He's an old, sad man, and he at least deserves some compassion.

"What have you done to the poor man?" Adam's voice grates, always when it's least possibly needed.

But Dr. Laurel looks towards the door like his salvation's come.

Because suddenly somehow I've become the bad guy in this scenario? For telling the truth? For trying to ostensibly get the company back on track to what Dr. Laurel always said he wanted for it?

But watching as Adam enters the room and takes Dr. Laurel under his broad, football arm and guides him out of the room, no doubt to his own car to drive him home and tuck him into bed—I can see the entire façade of charity driven by a cold-blooded desire to play to win.

The two of them fucking deserve each other.

But they think they can get rid of me that easy? They're dead fucking wrong. I'm not going to lie down and play dead. I'll be back bright and early tomorrow morning, a pin in their sides, a splinter underneath their finger...

But tonight?

I look down at my phone. No missed calls or new messages.

As much as I want to pretend all this doesn't affect me, it's a lie. I know myself. The pressure is building.

I need a release valve and I need it bad.

I haven't visited the dungeon in months. Long, long months.

But if I don't unwind some of this tension, it really will be ugly when I lash out. I stretch my neck this way and that, the first wave of calm settling over me as I begin to adopt the persona of *him*.

The Master.

But then all I can see is her face. *Daphne*.

What if I go by her place instead?

And do what? She might be 19, but she's still just a child. She's not ready for all I want to unleash. And with everything happening with her dad's company, is it really fair to put her in the middle of it?

Still, before I've even completely thought it through, I'm dialing her number and holding the phone to my ear. Lately it feels like she's the only person I can really talk to.

She doesn't pick up, though, and I hang up before I can hear her silken voice on the message again.

I lean back against the wall and drop the phone to my side. Probably for the best. I look around the darkened offices and a chill goes up my spine. I can't leave well enough alone. I need to have some sort of contact with her. She's my touchstone right now, though it might freak her out to know that.

But if Adam and her father have anything to do with it, she and I will never have the future I dream about together. If Dr. Laurel fires me and I don't get a chance to say goodbye to her, if Adam tries to poison them against me with his lies—

My fingers are on the phone, tapping out a text on the glowing screen in the otherwise darkened hallway. IF ANYTHING EVER HAPPENS, PLEASE KNOW YOU'RE MY BEST FRIEND. GIVE ME A CHANCE TO EXPLAIN. MEET ME AT THORNHILL, BESIDE YOUR MOM'S GRAVE. DON'T MEAN TO FREAK YOU OUT. JUST IN CASE ANYTHING EVER HAPPENS.

It's an ominous message and part of me feels regret at ever hitting send. But then again, it's been six months since her mother died. I'll give her all the time she needs and maybe she's not ready for everything I'm into, but...

I can't deny it anymore. My thoughts are full of her, night and day. Whenever she's ready, I want to try. I can go slow. As slow as she needs.

And in spite of everything, the terrible day, finding out

what a snake in the grass Adam is and Dr. Laurel turning out to be such a disappointment—I smile.

Because for the first time, I let myself dream of a future with her.

I fall asleep happy and I wake up happy.

In fact, I'm still smiling when I head into work and pull on my lab goggles the next morning.

I'm smiling until my skin starts burning.

Until I'm screaming and clawing at my face and begging for them to tear it off me. And what I mean by *it* is my own skin.

TWENTY-FIVE

Present Day
Daphne

My courage lasts for exactly six strides into the lushly appointed ballroom. There's so many people. All of New Olympus's high society, all in one room. Maybe if I just back out quietly, no one would even notice that I've—

But some wanker with a mic catches sight of me before I can make up my mind about retreating and announces, "Here she is! Adam Archer's fiancée and belle of the ball, Daphne Laurel!"

"*Doctor* Daphne Laurel," Rachel growls under her breath. "Just because a woman gets engaged doesn't mean she's stripped of all her titles."

I squeeze her hand, partly in gratitude, partly for support, and partly so she doesn't head off to strangle the stupid MC. The band strikes up a jazzed up version of

Wagner's "Bridal Chorus" that devolves after several bars into some sort of disco riff.

Hordes of glittering guests turn to greet me. Like a tennis match, all heads swing in my direction. There must be over a hundred people in the ballroom. I've never felt so exposed. I swallow my grimace at the music choices. At my side Rachel mutters, "Oh gods, disco? Why?" and pretends to gag.

"Rachel," I murmur through a gritted smile. "Will you be a dear and find my godsdamned fiancé?"

"Gladly, *Doctor* Laurel," she murmurs back and glides away. Once she's gone, I relax. I thought I'd want to put off meeting with Adam, but the sooner I drag him to a private meeting, the sooner I can end this farce. And then Rachel and I can take turns whipping him across the face with our opera gloves.

I fantasize about this for about three seconds before the first guest steps into my personal space. Fortunately, it's one of my favorite people. Cora Ubeli.

"Dr. Laurel," she hugs me like I'm a long lost friend from summer camp. When she steps back, huge diamonds at her ears and around her neck blind me. Her beauty is more striking than any bling she could wear, though.

She's the epitome of beauty, strength, and power. Dangerous power at that, if all the stories about her are to be believed, even though she's been nothing but kindness itself to me. But, for some reason I notice the wedding band on her ring finger has a dark red rock. The color of passion and blood, and anything but traditional, just like Cora and her intimidating husband themselves.

"Congratulations on everything," Cora gushes. She's stunning in a silvery blue sheath that complements her eyes. Her beauty is goddess-like, bright and stunning.

"Congratulations," her husband, Marcus Ubeli, echoes. He's the yin to Cora's yang, dark and handsome. A touch of grey at his temples only adds to his aura of prestige and power. Most of the people hovering around us probably want to talk to him instead of me.

"And where's your charming fiancé?" Cora asks, pretending to look behind me as if Adam is hiding there.

I wince. By not facing up to Adam sooner, I'm lying to these people. I hide my dismay but the way Cora's blue eyes rove over my face, I'm fooling no one. "Uh, we arrived separately. I've been holed up for a while, working on...a project." Because that's what I'm calling sex games with Logan. A project.

"Of course," Cora's gaze softens. She's going to let me off the hook. "You look so young, I forget you're a brilliant researcher." She catches my hand and squeezes it. I want to curl up in the warmth of her smile and purr like a cat. "The world needs you. But I hope you'll take some time off for yourself."

"Yes," Marcus hands his wife a flute of champagne. "Time off is important." He and Cora share a private look. "This building, for example. Did you know there's a floor dedicated to an art gallery?"

"Um, no. Adam chose it. I didn't get to explore it that much," I say.

"You should." His dark eyes twinkle. "There's a staircase and a fountain that's...quite fascinating."

Cora chokes on her champagne. Marcus puts a hand on her back and excuses them both. There's a lull while guests wait for the power couple to leave before rushing to greet me.

I staple a smile to my face and murmur *thanks* over and over. The guests fall into a few categories. There are older men with thinning hair and bespoke suits cut to hide their paunch who represent ninety-nine percent of New Olympus' net worth. A bevy of plastic looking celebrities whose smiles don't crease their Botoxed foreheads. Reporters in off-the-rack dress clothes who circle me slowly. I keep my comments vague about where I've been and what I've been doing. Any dropped hint would be blood in the water.

My throat is dry from fake-laughing and my face is sore from fake-smiling. Why did I ever dream about fitting in with these people? But I did. I saw this script for my life and I wanted to play the part written for me. Not that of the socialite. I was never going to be that.

But a respected CEO and researcher who hobnobs with the rich and influential? It was what my dad did and I assumed it was my path too. A respectable husband along the way was a given, just part of the picture that needed filling out so that my life was screen-ready.

But the truth is, all that takes is a robot. I could've stayed asleep my whole life and done exactly what they told me.

Without Logan, I might have let this all happen to me and only twenty years or more down the road had regrets about my hollow life and empty marriage.

A commotion behind me makes me turn.

It's Adam. My fiancé is surrounded by admirers. His hair is frosted like a singer in a boy band, and his smile is toothpaste-model white.

Did I ever think he was handsome? Or even cute? He's a plastic Ken doll compared to Logan's rugged good looks.

"There she is," Adam bursts out. As if he's surprised to see me at my own engagement ball. "My beautiful Daphne."

Inwardly I bristle. *Not yours.* But I take his hand and let the photographers swarm us. Behind them, I spot a fourth type of guest—flocks of stunning women, camera-ready with poreless skin and skin hugging dresses that leave them more naked than if they were actually naked. They alternate between gazing adoringly at Adam and shooting death glares at me. I barely stop myself from laughing.

Ladies, you can have him.

Adam pulls me too close—I've been careful of my nipple piercings so far, but the slightest brush against them is murder—and I suck in a breath and jerk back. "Careful."

"She's mad that I've been across the ballroom all night," Adam announces. His voice is louder than the MCs, and he doesn't even have a mic. Obnoxious much? "It's all right, sweetheart, I wasn't ignoring you. Give us a kiss."

Shit. Slapping him in the face would probably be a little too Real New Olympus Housewives and I didn't come here to make a scene. I don't want drama, I just want to end this and part ways cleanly. So I go up on tiptoe and peck him on his spray-tanned cheek. He's wearing too much cologne and I want to swipe at my face as soon as I pull away to get rid of the overwhelming scent.

"Oooh, playing hard to get," Adam makes the crowd chuckle. If I barf on him, I could claim food poisoning, right?

Adam has an arm around me, turning me this way and that. *Smile for the camera, Daphne. Show us your trophy.*

Only this time, I *am* the trophy.

"I need to talk to you. In private," I hiss to Adam, keeping a grin plastered to my face as the cameras blaze.

"Of course, darling." Adam coos, and adds for the crowd's benefit. "She wants to speak to me...alone." His voice drips with innuendo. Guests guffaw.

Fuck this. Fuck everyone. I grab Adams sleeve and

march ahead of him, through the foyer into a private room. The scent of store-bought roses is cloying.

"Daphne," Adam murmurs, shutting the door and swaying towards me.

I hold up a hand. "Adam, don't."

He chuckles. "It's all right. It's only me." He goes to the sideboard and pours champagne.

I tug off my glove and wriggle my bare fingers. *Deep breath.* I can do this.

"Let's toast," Adam says. "To us."

"In a minute. I have to speak to you."

Adam moves closer. When he looks down at my hand, his face goes blank. "Daphne, where's the ring?"

"I have it." I start to fumble in my purse like a child called on the carpet. Then I stop. What the hell am I doing, letting him put me on the defensive like this? "Adam, there's something I have to say first. Then, I'll give you back the ring."

His nostrils flare but I forge on. "I'm flattered that you proposed. I'm grateful that you tried to help me save face in front of the press. But I don't want this."

A rush of relief and empowerment sweeps through me as I finally say it.

My fingers find the ring and I hand it back to him. "You've been an ally of my father's company and a wonderful support to me and him. A friend. But I don't want to marry you."

There. I did it. I square my shoulders.

"Daphne," Adam murmurs, his voice dripping honey. His hand closes around mine, keeping the ring clenched in my fist. "You can't be serious."

My mouth drops open. I just stood tall and told him my truth and he's—

"I am serious," I protest. "Very serious. And look, I wanted to do this in private, to help you save face, but if you push it, I'll march out there and tell everyone."

And I will. He's not taking this away from me. No one is.

But while Adam can be obnoxious, he's not a bad guy. So I soften my voice, but only the slightest bit. He needs to know exactly how serious I am. "It might be better to wait a few months and work with a PR company to announce it quietly, but if you try to steamroll me, I'll just do it now with a mic." I tug my hand away and hold up the huge diamond. Then I say it again, and say it firmly. "I don't want to get married."

"All right," he says carefully, and steps back. He gets it. I can see he doesn't like it, but he gets it. "If that's what you want."

"It is." There's a moment I almost fumble the ring, but it lands safely in Adam's palm and he tucks it away. The knuckles of his fist are white and his jaw is a tightly clenched, but he doesn't argue.

I blow out a huge breath. I did it and I feel like I've lost twenty thousand pounds of extra weight.

I want to kick off my heels and head home, but the party isn't over. Even though all I want to do is call a car service, drive back to the castle, and throw myself in Logan's arms in victory.

But being strong isn't just a one-time occurrence. Now comes the real test, going out and being strong in front of all those strangers out there.

Really, it doesn't sound so scary anymore. Apart from a few people like the Ubelis, I couldn't care less about the people out there. Who cares what they think of me? This is my life and it's time to live the fuck out of it.

"Shall we go out and mingle with the guests?" I ask Adam. "If anyone asks the wedding date, we just tell them we're going to wait awhile. We have a lot going on with our companies." I offer Adam a smile. It costs me nothing to be nice.

For a second he says nothing. His head is bowed and face is in shadow, his hand still in his pocket. Playing with the ring?

Then he grabs a glass of champagne from the sidebar and steps close, flashing the charming smile paparazzi know and love.

"Of course," he replies smoothly. "Champagne? I ordered the best. Might as well enjoy it." Up close, his face is stunning, but his eyes are flat. His smile has no soul.

I sip the drink not because I want it, but because I want to make him feel better. He is a friend, especially to my father. Maybe I should've let him down more gently. "Adam, I—"

"We should get back," he cuts me off, heading to the door. Fair enough. Before he gets there, it opens and a man in a suit walks in. He's burly and has one of those clear earpieces, so he's probably security.

"Sir, we have a visitor. An uninvited guest. He's pushed his way inside and is demanding to speak with you."

"I'm coming," Adam promises. "Daphne?" He holds out his hand to me.

I ignore it and glide past him. The security guard and Adam both flank me as I stride through the foyer.

One more hour of glad-handing, and I'll make my excuses and go. Considering travel time...that means probably one hour and twenty-five minutes until I can be back in Logan's bed. I grin. I'll count down the minutes. He'll be so proud of me for tonight.

I grin, feeling lit up from the inside out. I'll have to come up with some *very* creative ways to reward him for finally trusting me and—

"There he is, sir," the security guard mutters to Adam as we enter the ballroom.

Ahead there's a mountain of a man standing at the bar. He turns his dark head and light catches on his white mask.

No.

I stop dead on the marble floor and Adam bumps into me, making me stagger. But I don't take my eyes off Logan.

Logan.

It's definitely him, in a black tuxedo and a white mask.

The bartender and guests huddle away from him. Other than sidelong glances, they give him a wide berth. He stands with a glass swallowed in his fist, tension and menace emanating from his huge form, a second away from ripping off his tuxedo and attacking the room with a roar. As if he's truly the Beast he calls himself.

The high I was riding crashes hard.

He promised. He said I could do this. I thought he'd let me handle this alone, make my own choices.

My hand flies to my chest because it hurts. It *hurts*. Like I fell out of a tree and all the air's been knocked out of me.

Why, oh why couldn't he trust me?

"Well, well, well," Adam swaggers up to the bar. *No,* I want to scream. Can't he see Logan's unpredictable? Maybe even dangerous? "Love the mask. But you missed the memo. This is a private event. And you aren't invited."

Logan's lip curls. He looms over Adam, stripping him down with a gaze. "You told me once I'd be your best man, Archer. Then again, that was before you stole my work and tried to kill me."

I gasp and take a step back. Of course I've known for a

while about Logan's accusations and vendetta but the fact that he's using this venue, *this* moment, to air his grievances and confront Adam, after all these years—

Around us, the party rolls on. The DJ is inviting people to dance. Some of Adam's groupies have noticed the tense showdown though.

For the first time tonight, Adam Archer looks unsure. Then he brays a laugh. His sycophants chuckle nervously along with him. "Oh, this is too good. Logan Wulfe. Back from the dead. I have to say, man, you look like shit. Didn't you have a run in with flesh-eating bacteria a while back?"

"No thanks to you," Logan rasps, but his neck flushes dark red.

He's not even looking at me.

All he can see is Adam. And his revenge.

Adam rolls his eyes, playing to the crowd. "You were always obsessed with me. You'd think you'd take a hint when I filed a restraining order. We were friends once, but you can't ride the coattails of my success forever. A grown man, still doing the professional equivalent of cheating off his best friend's homework? It was pathetic. I did you a favor when I cut you loose."

"I cheated off you? That's not how I remember it."

I watch it all play out in front of me like a train wreck.

"The evidence says otherwise," Adam's voice is sharp as a knife. He might be outmatched in a fist fight, but he's a powerful enemy.

"You stole the company, my reputation, and my research. And then you tried to kill me." Logan's giant fist closes around the whiskey glass until it cracks. Adam and I wince. "Did you think I would just lay down and take it?"

Adam shrugs, but he's taken several steps back and signaled to security. "You always were a dog."

"And you always were a worm," Logan booms loud enough to overpower the MC. The guests around us gasp. "You stole from me. Left me for dead. Left me to plan your downfall."

Adam's face is a grotesque mask, a hideous smile fixed to his lips that doesn't touch his eyes.

"Now I steal your fiancée." And Logan holds out his hand to me. "Daphne, come."

As if I'm a dog. Or more like the bone between two dogs. Just another kind of trophy. In this moment, I feel like an object Logan wants just for bragging rights over his rival. Was that what this was always about? Did he only seek me out me now because Adam was showing an interest in me? How dare he make me feel so small?

I don't move.

"Daphne," Adam says silkily. I shoot him a furious glare and he stops in his tracks. He knows if he pushes me, I'll announce the end of our engagement in front of everyone. That's what Logan wants me to do, but fuck him. Fuck all of them.

I shake my head. This wasn't how it was supposed to be. I was supposed to be free to choose. Free. I was supposed to be *free*. But once again, Logan took away all my choices. And why? To make me a pawn in his stupid game.

Because it was never about me.

It was always about his revenge.

The music has stopped. The whole ballroom is focused on us. The reporters don't know what's going on, but half of them are on their phones. They'll get private detectives to dig, and it'll be six hours before the whole mess breaks as news on the internet.

My hands are fisted at my sides. I raise my chin. *Fuck*

you, Logan. He wants to force me to choose him or Adam? I'm done playing this game.

I choose myself.

Without a word, I turn on my heel and walk out of the ballroom.

TWENTY-SIX

Present Day
Logan

She. Left. Me. The ballroom tilts and the colors spin.

I was sitting back at the castle, planning to stay out of it like I said I would. But then all the old memories came back. As much as I trust her, I sure as hell don't trust Adam Archer. He's tricked and manipulated everyone around him his whole life.

He's dangerous. The son of a bitch almost *killed* me.

How could I let her walk into the wolf's den all alone? Who knows what he might have done to her when she rejected him? She was in *physical danger*. I couldn't stay back. I'm the only one who knows what he's truly capable of. I had to protect her.

But then everything got so out of control. I finally unmasked Adam but it didn't go like I always planned.

She didn't rush into my arms.

No, she ran the other way.

You're a monster. Of course she ran, especially when others were looking on.

In front of me, Adam is shouting something. A phalanx of security guards in penguin suits rush me. I push them off, heading to the door. But she's already gone. Gone, gone, gone.

This foyer is covered in roses. Red and white and rose, but all I see is green. The color of emeralds. Of absinthe. Of poison.

The color of her eyes. Daphne, the goddess in a green dress. She was so lovely—and untouchable.

I wanted to kneel at her feet. I don't deserve her. The son of a strung out mother and a father who never claimed me. A bastard in every sense of the word.

Cruel hands grab me and I fight on autopilot. There are too many, and they drag me down the stairs. The basement air is full of mold. Of course. A beautiful building, rotting from the inside. New Olympus in a nutshell.

A shadow steps in front of me. This is going to hurt.

A punch to the face. Another. They want me to pay for breathing their air. For existing. I smile through aching teeth, dripping blood.

"Hit him again." Adam says, excited. He sounds like he has a hard-on from seeing me bleed.

I throw off the men holding me. Four on one, and they can't keep me down.

"You," I snarl in Adam's direction. He doesn't look scared. He holds all the cards. He always did. Fucker's been playing me since he met me. A poor, scrawny kid on scholarship.

I played the cards I had and...I dealt wrong. Daphne's gone. Have I lost her for good this time?

"Logan," Adam says. "You came back."

"I never left."

"I always wondered what happened to you. The hospital told me you disappeared, but I didn't follow up."

"This isn't over," I promise, and head for the back door. I'll find Daphne, get her back. Keep her safe while I destroy her father and Adam, my enemies.

The battle is lost, but the war? The war has just begun.

TWENTY-SEVEN

Present Day
Daphne

I'm shaking as the cab pulls away from the curb. No one spills out of the ballroom to follow me. Not even Logan.

I half expect him to burst out of the building and chase down the car like a monster in a movie. Part of me wants him to. The other part of me is pissed. I'd cross my arms over my chest, but I don't want to chafe my nipples. Although, I laughed bitterly, what do the piercings even matter anymore?

The cab turns the corner, heading to my apartment at the heart of the city, and suddenly I'm super cold.

The ring is gone, and with it a huge weight. If tonight had gone as planned, I'd be heading back to the castle. Back to Logan, my Master. Why did he have to ruin everything? I was his. The big stupid dominant nerd.

I. Was. His. Did I have to brand his initials on my butt for him to know it?

The woman reflected in the cab window smiles sadly. She's stunningly beautiful, but looks so alone. I fought hard and have come so far, only to end up alone.

"It's not fair," I growl at her.

"Excuse me, miss?" the cabbie asks.

"Um, nothing." I duck my head. Great, now I'm a crazy woman, talking to herself in the backseat of a hired car.

If only Logan had trusted me. Now he thinks I left him, when really I was trying to return to him with no strings attached. Completely free. It's not fair that he chased me down, but when is life fair? Love is not just give and take. The more I give, the more I own his heart.

I sit up straight on the tattered backseat. Maybe that's it.

Maybe I've done all I can do and it's up to him. All I can do is control my own actions and continue down this path, wherever it leads me.

What do I *want*? What do *I* really want? Not my father, not the board, not Adam, and not even Logan?

What do I want and what am I willing to sacrifice to get it? *The gods won't accept a small sacrifice,* my father once told me. *They want everything.* He was old and tired after my mother's last relapse. Her disease was taking its toll, taking it all, but he was willing to give up everything for love.

He was even willing to sacrifice me, his daughter.

But he's no role model and I'm not him. I won't abandon my soul so that love contorts until it looks nothing like love.

Who am I, Daphne? What is core to what makes up me and what will I sacrifice for that true self I'm only just discovering?

The past month has shown that I'm willing to give up a

lot of external things I thought defined me and only then have I been stripped down enough to discover who I really am. Maybe I need to sacrifice it all if Logan and I are really going to have a chance. Because it's ultimately what I'm asking of him, isn't it? To choose me over his revenge.

"Miss? We're here."

I pay the driver and tumble from the cab. I'm still shaking with adrenaline and cold, but I don't feel so empty.

Maybe that's the answer. The ultimate sacrifice to the gods. I can give up everything. And be completely free.

I skip up the stairs and put the key in the lock of my apartment door, ready for a long, hot soak in my bathtub.

But when I push my door open, my apartment is...empty.

And I mean, completely freaking empty. We're talking bare walls and bare floors. There's not even a living room rug left. Or a lamp. It's all gone.

"What the f—"

"I tried to tell you before you left the ball."

I spin around, mouth open, to find Rachel standing behind me, her cheeks flushed and chest heaving. Her normally perfect bun askew. "I chased after you but you'd already gotten in the taxi."

"Why didn't you tell me *before*? We spent hours together while I was getting ready!"

She drops her eyes. "I don't know. I guess I thought maybe you and Adam would work it out and it wouldn't matter."

"What does *Adam* have to do with this?"

"He's the one who moved all your stuff into his place. As like, a surprise engagement present."

Adam fucking Archer. What the hell is up with him? Did he always just stampede over people and then pretend it was a 'present' or a 'surprise' or was it only with women he was supposedly engaged to?

The gods want everything. But Adam isn't a god. He's a spoiled rich boy.

My hands are in my hair as if I'm about to rip it out by the roots. I force myself to let go, lower my hands and huff out a long breath. "This is so not okay. Where am I going to sleep tonight?" There's zero furniture left in my townhouse. Just a dust outline of where my pictures used to hang on the wall. *Fucking Adam Archer.*

"You know what? Fuck this. I'm going to sleep in my own damn apartment. Come on. Let's go get my stuff from Adam's. You game?"

Rachel looks uncertain. "I don't know. It's so late already."

I pull my phone out of my small clutch. "It's only nine forty-five. And I don't even have pajamas to change into here!"

Rachel bites her lip. "I'd say you could come back to my place but the guy I've been seeing has been staying over a lot and he'll be there tonight..."

And now I feel like crap. "Oh Rachel." I grab her hands. "I'm such a shit. You've got your whole life going on and a new guy and I haven't even asked you about it. I swear I'm going to start being a better friend."

She squeezes my hand and smiles wanly. "It's okay. Really. Don't worry about it. The new guy isn't that serious."

"But he's staying at your place all the time?"

She waves it away. "Let's go get your stuff. One drama at a time."

I frown at my friend. Usually whenever she's got a new

man I can barely shut her up, she wants to analyze and dissect every single thing he's said and done. But she's bailing me out big time helping me tonight so I won't push it.

"Come on," she says, "I'll told my cabbie to wait for me. I didn't think you'd want to stay here."

I nod and we hurry downstairs. I feel a little ridiculous running around town in my elaborate ballgown and updo, but whatever.

I'm taking back my life, dammit, and it starts now. With me sleeping on my own bed, with my own sheets and my own pillows.

Rachel's quiet on the ride over. And again I feel like a crappy friend for monopolizing our friendship lately and not paying more attention to what's going on in her life lately. I've been taking her for granted, and if there's one thing I want to do better in my new life, it's to value the people in life who matter.

Adam's high-rise is next to the Crown hotel, and built to match the hotel's famous white and gold style. All the Who's Who of New Olympus have a permanent residence here.

"Wait for us, we won't be long," I start to tell the cabbie, but then Rachel jolts and says, "No, don't wait."

I frown at her but she says quickly, "We'll just catch another cab. It might take awhile to gather your stuff together."

Okay, fair enough. And cabs aren't too hard to find in this part of town so we pay the cabbie and then walk into the lush white marble-lined lobby. My steps falter at the line of beefy security guards blocking the elevator. But Rachel knows just what to do.

"Can I help you, ma'am?" the doorman asks.

"We need apartment 32D," Rachel leans in and flutters her lashes. "Adam Archer's residence. He's expecting us."

"Of course, ma'am. One moment." The doorman puts a phone to his ear. If he's wondering why we're in ballgowns with opera gloves, he doesn't comment.

I sidle up to Rachel. "What are you doing?"

"Buzzing Adam. He'll let us in." She seems so confident.

"Is he here?"

"The party broke up soon after you left." I can see she wants to ask me more questions, but the doorman interrupts.

"Apartment 32D. Right this way," he escorts us past security to the elevators and types in a code with a white-gloved finger. Rachel thanks him prettily, but I've fallen silent. The mirrored elevator wall shows two disheveled debutantes.

I gnaw on my lip for thirty one of the thirty two floors. Will this send the wrong message to Adam, me coming here right after I broke off the engagement? Whatever, I'll set him straight soon enough. He's pulled multiple dick moves and it's time to start setting things straight. Or rather, continue setting things straight. I started things off right at the ball and it's time to continue taking back my own life.

Besides, Rachel's here so it's not like he can try anything funny. I shake my head even at the thought. Adam's harmless. I know Logan hates him and has the elaborate conspiracy theory about him having some part in Logan's terrible accident, but Adam's like a tamed house cat—all the lion has been domesticated out of him through millennia of careful cultivation.

Adam opens the door with a wide smile on his face that

doesn't even dim when he sees Rachel beside me. "Ladies, welcome." He gestures us into his apartment.

I steel my spine. "Adam, I'm just here to get my stuff back. It wasn't cool that you moved it without even telling me."

He nods but just keeps gesturing us inside. "I understand. I was just trying to make everything special for you when you were under so much stress, but I can see how it could be considered overstepping. I'm sorry. Look, Daphne, I'm sorry for everything. Please. Come in."

I blink. Okaaaaaaaay, wow. I didn't expect a genuine apology. For the first time all night, the plastic mask of his boyish good looks has cracked and I feel like there's genuine emotion shining through his eyes.

I nod slowly and step inside Adam's apartment.

My stuff is everywhere, mixed in with his. My lamps are artfully nested amongst his modern, angular furniture, giving a softening, feminine touch to the place. My art is mounted along the walls.

I don't know whether to be flattered or creeped out.

Maybe if we were a real couple, genuinely in love... But we never were. Never even close. Did Adam think that was real love? A real relationship?

Compared to the intimacy I've found with Logan, that's sad if he did.

Logan. Even thinking his name makes my chest clench. He hurt me tonight by not believing in me when he said he would. If he can't trust me, then how can we ever—

"Here, let me get you a drink, and then I'll help you gather your stuff together."

"No, really, Adam, you don't have to—" I start, but he's already disappeared into the kitchen. But he doesn't come back with champagne or anything like that, just two glasses of ice water, one for Rachel and one for me.

It's thoughtful and I actually am really thirsty, so I take a long, deep sip. "Thanks, Adam."

"Here's the suitcase with your clothes. You can change while we start packing."

Wow. He's actually being decent about this. I nod and roll the suitcase he pointed out to the guestroom. As I close the door, I hear him and Rachel start to make small talk.

Unzipping the suitcase, I sort through the clothes, frowning when I see all my underthings among the other clothes. Good gods, did he pack this? The brief image of him in my apartment, hands in my underwear drawer sends a creepy chill down the back of my neck.

But then I shake it off. That doesn't seem like the kind of manual labor Adam Archer would be into. No doubt he had some assistant do it. Let's just hope it was a female assistant.

Quickly I unzip my dress and step out of it, slipping on some yoga pants and a loose t-shirt instead.

Rachel and Adam's voices immediately quiet as soon as I open the door again and come back out into the living room. Adam's assembling a cardboard box and Rachel has plucked a couple of paintings off the wall that she knows are mine.

"I won't be able to get it all tonight, obviously." I look around. "And what did you do with my couch and my mattress?"

"Storage," Adam says, looking up.

Son of a—

"Why would you *do* that without talking to me, Adam?"

He straightens up after taping the box. "I was trying to be romantic."

I huff out an exasperated breath. Okay, so we're going to finally have this out. "Romantic would have been talking to me. Planning an engagement party *with* me. Not going behind my back and doing all this stuff when I didn't even want it."

"It wasn't behind your back. I would have done it with you. If you'd been here."

"Ever think there was a reason I wasn't here?" I retort before I can think better of it. But screw it. Why should I have to walk around on eggshells just to protect his fragile ego? This is bullshit.

I run a hand through my hair and sigh. "Look, I'm just saying that if two people aren't communicating, then that's a big red flag. You should have tried harder to talk to me before things went as far as they did."

Adam's mouth tightens. "I was worried about you."

I'm about to balk but then he comes close. "What are you doing, Daphne? I was trying to give you a way forward to keep Belladonna. This is what you've wanted your whole life."

I open my mouth, then frown. I mean, yes, Belladonna has been my life. But is it the life I chose?

Wasn't I just thinking that I'd be willing to sacrifice anything if it meant moving forward in this new freedom?

What if...what if I let Belladonna go?

I freeze at the impossibility of the idea. The thought is like a huge chasm yawning before me. But a few ideas immediately take form. Even without Belladonna, I can still pursue research. I'd be leaving Rachel, but we could still be friends. We could hang out—*gasp*—outside of work! And I could get more friends. For the first time in my life, I could have a life.

No more board trying to dictate my actions.

No more of Logan's second-guessing my motives. It hasn't been about the patents for a long time for me but finally, he wouldn't have to doubt that. It might remove the last barrier to him trusting me.

I could do what I love, which is being down in the lab doing research, not the grind and glad-handing of being CEO, all of which I hate.

If tonight's proven anything, it's that I'm a new Daphne. The old one doesn't fit the mold anymore. That's what I've been learning in my time with Logan—that there's *more* to life, more to *me*, than just the quiet, obedient daughter who does what she's supposed to.

It's all on the tip of my tongue. *I'm a new Daphne,* I want to say. But I feel myself shrinking under Adam and Rachel's stares.

Not to mention that the room is strangely blurry. I put a hand to my head. I haven't taken out my contacts yet, but the shadows on the wall seem to stretch, swallowing everything up.

What was I just thinking about? Right, Belladonna. "I don't know if I want that anymore."

"Really? What would your father say?" Adam asks, brow still furrowed in concern. "Battleman's was his life's fight. For the sake of the gods', Daphne, what would your *mother* say?"

His words hit me with the weight of a freight train and I stumble back a step.

"Adam, that's not fair," Rachel starts but he holds up a hand to quiet her.

"I'm serious. Daphne, you've fought your whole life to save others like her. Are you going to give up on everyone else who's sick just because, what?" he scoffs. "You don't feel like it anymore?"

I shake my head, but everything that was so clear only moment ago has started to become fuzzy. "No, I- That's, I- I would never give up on Battleman's—" I put a hand on my hand and blink hard.

And then, as I'm looking at him, suddenly the world swoops sideways as a wave of dizziness hits me out of nowhere.

I grab for the wall, only barely catching myself as Rachel rushes to my side. "Daphne, are you okay?" she cries.

I blink hard but when I look up, there are two of her, then three, all dancing around. The dizziness only gets worse the more I blink and try to get my bearings. "I don't feel so good," I mutter as she helps me to the couch.

"How much did she drink at the ball?" Adam asks, sounding appalled.

I open my mouth to say I barely drank two sips of champagne at the ball but no sound comes out. Everything's gone so blurry and liquid around me.

"Here, help me get her to the guest bedroom," Adam says. "She can sleep it off there."

The world goes even crazier, dipping and swooping, as Adam lifts me up in his arms and Rachel hurries near, her voice murmuring low words I can't quite make out.

EVERYTHING'S MOVING SO slow but when I blink and look around, I think it's a long while later, maybe even an hour or two.

Loud voices make me blink to alertness. I don't think I was asleep exactly, more like just really, really out of it.

Something's wrong. Really wrong. When I try to sit up or move my arms, they don't respond right.

It's like I've...like I've been *drugged*.

Holy shit. Holy shit...

The thought should be scary. It means I could be in danger. But it feels really detached. Far away.

Rachel's here. She won't let anything bad happen to me.

The door of the bedroom bursts open and a giggling Rachel comes in, her arms wrapped around Adam's neck. *What?*

I blink puffy eyes, sure what I'm seeing can't be right. The only light is from the window and the hallway, casting long shadows.

"Come on," Rachel says. "It's enough that she's spending the night. We don't have to do anything more."

"Don't be a bitch. Help me get her clothes off."

That voice doesn't sound anything like the Adam I know. It was mean. All his careful gentility is gone.

"Fine," Rachel sighs, "but just her top. That's all you'll need for the pictures."

"Whatever," Adam says as they both move closer to me.

Run. *Run. Escape.*

But my arms and legs barely respond and the only thing that comes out of my mouth is a low groan.

"You hear that?" Adam laughs nastily. "She wants it. She's practically begging for it."

"Don't be an ass." Rachel comes over and shoves Adam out of the way, sitting on the bed beside me. I try desperately to make eye-contact with her but she studiously avoids looking at my face as she lifts me up enough to pull my t-shirt off over my head.

I'm left in the red lingerie I was wearing under my ballgown as she settles me back onto the pillows.

"Fuck, her nipples are pierced," Adam mutters. "I knew she was hot, didn't know she had a wild side."

I can't move my hands to cover my breasts but my shoulders hunch.

"Let's just snap some pics and then leave her alone."

"Don't be such a buzzkill."

The bed dips again and thick, cloying cologne wafts over me. Shivers crawl down my spine. It's him. Adam. The man I completely misjudged. The monster behind the handsome prince's mask. Gods, how could I have been so stupid as to come here tonight.

And Rachel... I search her out with my heavy eyes. She's got her back turned as Adam climbs into bed with me.

When she finally turns around, she's holding her phone.

"Okay, let's do this."

My confused brain takes a second to make sense out of the obvious, and it's not until Adam pulls me against his bare chest, settling my hand against his too-pale skin and a camera flash goes off that it finally clicks.

They're taking pictures of me. *Naked pictures.*

I want to scratch Adam's eyes out and kick him in the balls. And then tear Rachel's hair out by her pretty blonde roots.

Instead, all I can do is give confused, disagreeing moans as Adam moves me this way and that, moving my hair to get the best shot of my face, sometimes cupping my face, all the time making me want to barf on his overly waxed chest.

"Okay, that's enough," Rachel announces. "Let's go back to your bedroom."

"I don't know," Adam murmurs, running his hand down my chest and squeezing me. "I think we could have a lot of fun right here. You know how much I like them quiet and willing like this."

"She's not willing, she's out of it." Rachel's voice is sharp, but then it softens. "But baby, I'll do anything you want." She moves behind Adam and starts to massage his shoulders. "I'll suck you off. And I know you've been wanting to stick it up my ass. I'll let you tonight. Just leave her alone."

Finally Adam moves and his weight disappears from the mattress beside me. "You'll let me? You'll fucking let me?" His angry voice fills the room, echoing around my pounding head. "Have you forgotten how this arrangement works? You do what I fucking ask. And yes, I'll take your ass. I'll take it right here where she watches."

But at that point, finally, blessedly, I pass out.

TWENTY-EIGHT

Present Day
Daphne

Oh fuck, my *head*. I wake up, grabbing my head in my hands and squinting against the sunlight. What hellacious things did I do to my body last night?

Which is when I look around.

Wait up. Where the *hell* am I?

I jerk out of bed and get to my feet.

Mistake, mistake!

I grab my head and double over, feeling so nauseous I'm shocked I don't lose my stomach right there by the side of the bed.

When I finally manage to make it to the attached bathroom, I sit hugging the toilet bowl for another ten minutes, and finally splash my face with cool water when the worst of it has passed.

Bits and pieces of last night come back to me, but most of it is a huge blank.

I remember Rachel and I coming over to Adam's place. Adam and I were arguing. He said I was letting my Mom and Dad down. I cradle my queasy stomach as I try to remember what happened next.

I started feeling bad and Adam asked how much I'd had to drink at the party. He and Rachel helped me to the bedroom...

Then there's just...*nothing*.

Nothing till I woke up a few minutes ago.

I brush my teeth with a spare toothbrush and throw on a t-shirt, then head out to the rest of the apartment to see if I can make more sense of what happened. "Adam? Hello? Rachel?"

But the place is empty. When I wander into the kitchen, there's a note. Didn't want to wake you, sleepyhead. There's coffee in the carafe and some bagels and muffins. Help yourself to anything. I meant what I said last night. I was just trying to make your dreams come true. I hope we can talk more soon, Adam.

I stare at the note for a moment longer. It's so friendly and fits in with everything I know about Adam...but something feels...*off*. I can't explain it.

All I know is I don't want to be here anymore. I shake my head and slip into my athletic shoes, then pull two heavy suitcases of my clothes behind me as I hit the elevators and head downstairs.

It's easy to catch a cab since Adam's place is downtown and soon I'm on my way home. I'll have to call a moving truck this weekend to get the rest of my stuff from Adam's and from wherever he put it in storage.

And then what? What comes next?

Logan. Everything got so crazy last night I've barely had two minutes to think about him, but he's got to be hurting right now. But he's got to understand that I wasn't rejecting *him* last night, just his high-handedness. In the bedroom, yes, I love it. He commands and I obey and in a wild way I still don't fully understand, it's allowed me to be free. But our relationship only works if we trust each other.

I need him to trust me as absolutely as I trust him.

I take a deep breath as I let my head sink back on the seat cushion.

"Hey, I know you," the cabbie suddenly says. "You're famous. You're all over the papers today."

"What?" I lift my head up and frown at him.

He's squinting at the rearview mirror, sizing me up. "Holy shit, it really is you. Wait till I tell my buddies, they won't believe it."

We come to stop at a red light and he pulls out his phone. "You mind posing for a pic? Otherwise the guys'll never believe I drove you around."

"Wait, what do you mean, I was in the papers—" but he's already snapping away.

"Stop it," I hold out my hand as the car behind us honks its horn. The light's turned green.

The cabbie drops his phone and starts driving again. Seriously, what the hell? Was my broken engagement to Adam in the papers today? Do the gossip rags really not have better to report on?

"So were they your idea or Archer's?"

"What?"

"The piercings," he points to my chest. "Wouldn't have pegged you as that sort of girl."

Who does this guy think he is? I start to pull out headphones so I can listen to music for the rest of the ride, but not before I hear him add, "The two of you looked cozy in bed."

My head snaps up. In bed?

"What are you talking about?"

"Pics in *The New Olympian Inquirer*. You and Archer all hot and heavy. Everyone in the city's talking about it."

What. The. Fuck.

I stuff my earbuds in for the last ten minutes and give a minimal tip when he drops me off at my townhouse. What kind of crap have they photoshopped now just to sell that gossip rag? I hurry over to a newsstand close to my building, still dragging my two heavy suitcases behind me as I go.

I don't have to look hard to find it. The paper is front and center, the headline above the fold reading, "Mogul Adam Archer's Engagement: The Inside Story" and smaller, *Insider snaps of couple canoodling after their big celebration.*

I snatch the paper off the stand. It's me. I don't know how, but it's *me*. In the red bra I'm still wearing now. I'm lying sprawled across Adam's chest, in my bra, in a bed.

What. The. FUCK?

"Hey lady, you gotta pay for that. You're mangling it all up!"

I rip the paper down. It is indeed mangled in my clenched hands. Mouth pursed in fury, I fumble in my purse for some cash and slap it down on the counter of the little kiosk, then I spin away and look at the paper. There's not just one picture, there's several. It's clearly me. In only one of the pictures are my eyes open the slightest crack, but I look super out of it.

Which confirms the suspicion that's been niggling on

the edge of my mind all morning. It was just so absurd, I didn't think there was any *way*—

But it's terribly clear now.

I was drugged.

I was fucking drugged last night.

At the engagement party? At Adam's?

Did *Adam Archer* drug me?

Even as I think it, it sounds absolutely ludicrous. He's New Olympus's golden boy. Heir to a billion dollar empire.

But I've been drugged before...and this felt eerily similar. And Adam was at the Autumnal Ball. So was Logan. And a lot of other people were at both events, for that matter.

I rub a hand at my pounding temple. Then another terrifying thought strikes. Did anything else happen to me while I was unconscious? But I squeezed my thighs together and do a quick inventory of my body and nothing feels off or like it was...invaded. At least physically.

But how in the hell did the paper get the pictures? I look back down. Adam looks asleep in the pictures, too. So who took them? What the *hell* is going on?

All I know is that it's time to get some answers. I'm tired of being in the dark.

I hold up my hand and call, "Taxi!"

"SHE INSISTED SHE SEE YOU, SIR," Adam's harried assistant follows after me when I barge into Adam's office. His corner office is on the top floor of Archer Industries, as spare and masculine as his apartment.

There are several other men in suits opposite Adam's

massive desk but he waves to his assistant. "It's all right, Gladys. If you'll excuse me, gentleman, I'll need to conclude this meeting early. I have a pressing appointment."

Adam nods my way as the gentleman get up and gather their things, immediately at his beck and call.

Adam walks over towards me, blond hair styled to perfection. "I've been trying to call you all day. Are you okay?"

I frown at the concern in his eyes. He seems absolutely genuine but something makes me shiver. I don't know why goosebumps suddenly run up and down my arms at his proximity.

"You have?" I pull out my phone, only now realizing it's dead.

"I've had my publicist trying to get ahead of it. I can't believe Rachel would do this to us."

I blink. "Wait, *what?* Rachel?"

Adam stares at me a moment, before saying slowly, "What do you *think* happened last night?"

He urges me to come in and take a seat. I feel a little like I'm being herded, but I do sit down.

He offers me a bottle of water. For a second I stare at it, remembering when he offered me water last night.

"I think I was drugged," I finally say, carefully watching his reaction.

He wipes a hand down his face and looks towards the window before softly cursing. "I can't believe she would go that far...but you did seem out of it. When you wandered into my room, it was like you were sleepwalking but I couldn't wake you up. You just climbed into bed with me and it seemed better to just let you rest there."

His head snaps back to me, hands up. "I was a perfect

gentleman. I didn't do anything. We just slept. But Rachel must have come in at some point and taken those horrible pictures. And gods, if she *drugged* you to make you so out of it just so she could get the shots..."

I shake my head. "None of what you're saying makes any sense. Why would Rachel do any of that? She's my best friend."

Adam cocks his head to the side. "Is she? I've gotten to know her a little in the past few weeks while you were out of town, to help me with planning and coordinating meetings with Belladonna." Adam reaches out and puts a hand on my thigh. It feels wrong and I pull away. It could just be because anyone besides Logan touching me feels wrong. Adam lets me pull away without comment, then continues on about Rachel.

"To me, it's felt like she's jealous of you. She complained about how you're always getting all the attention, even when you weren't there. She said your friendship was always about you and never about her. I don't know, I can only guess. But it was definitely her who sold the pictures to the *Inquirer*. I had my people look into it. Maybe it was just for the money. She sold them for half a million dollars."

All the air heaves out of my lungs at his words. Half a million dollars? Holy shit. That's enough money to tempt anybody.

But still, *Rachel*? I've known her for years. I thought we were...friends.

Though maybe that was all in my head. Maybe in reality I was just her boss who she put up with because, well, I was paying her salary. And when a better opportunity came along...

I stand up and turn away from Adam. "I need to go."

It's time for that long, hot bath I never got. I need some time to clear my head and try to untangle the truth from fiction. If that's even possible at this point.

TWENTY-NINE

22 Years Ago
Logan

"Yeah, you better run! Run home to mommy!"

I flee up the steps of my trailer home and make it inside right as a rock hits the door behind me. Bastards!

I slam the door shut and put my back against it, breathing hard. They'll leave me alone now that I'm home, but it's really only putting it off until tomorrow.

Caleb, Pete, and Pete's brother Paul are these giant assholes from school who live in the same trailer park but have somehow decided they're better than me. Really there's just *more* of them and Pete got held back a year so they're all giant fucks even though we're all just twelve.

I thunk my head back against the flimsy wooden barrier. But at least for tonight, I'm safe.

I have to blink to see around the double-wide, Mom

keeps it so dark in here. I can immediately tell she hasn't been out to look for a job like she promised.

She's stuck in the same place on the couch where I left her this morning when I took off for school, nestled with about a thousand blankets over her, zoned out to what's on TV.

"Have you eaten?" I start to ask when I notice a new addition to the discarded packages of chips and TV dinners.

"Mom," I say slowly. "Why are all your pills out on the table like that?" There are dozens of bottles all grouped together, beside a tall glass of water.

It's like for the first time since I banged into house she even realizes I'm home. "Oh, Logan. I didn't hear you come in."

It's then that I really take in my mom. She used to be really pretty. I've seen pictures. But now she just looks…old and tired. Her eyes are sunken and barely open. Her hair is kind of papery and fried from being bleached too many times.

She was doing okay last year when she had this boyfriend, Rog, but he was a loser like every other guy she chooses and after they broke up, she's just never really recovered.

When my dad left when I was little, she tried to kill herself. She wears bracelets on her wrists to cover the marks, but I never forget they're there.

I eye all the little bottles again, wanting to grab them all up and pour them down the kitchen sink.

"Mom," I insist. "What are you doing?"

Her eyes drift back towards me. "I don't really understand the point of it all anymore. Why we're all trying so hard. For what?"

For me! I want to grab her shoulders and scream. *For your fucking son!*

Why can she find the point in living for all those boyfriends but never for me? I guess I'm not enough. Was never enough.

I clench my jaw and stubbornly move past her to the coffee table and start gathering up all the little pill bottles.

"Wait, what are you doing?" It's the first time all afternoon I've heard any life in her. "Stop that. Logan, I need those."

I spin on her. "For what? So you can kill yourself and leave me all alone?"

She looks hurt, like I've wounded her, but then her eyes drop guiltily. Because we both know I've just spoken the truth. "It's not like that, Logan. It's not about you. These are grown-up problems. You can't underst—"

"And if you die and leave me alone? You think that's not some grown-up shit I'll have to deal with?"

"Logan," she gasps. "Language."

"See?" I take her hands. "I need my mom to get on my case about language. I need you, Mom. I love you. It's us against the world, right?"

She nods wobbly and squeezes my hands back.

"So you won't leave me?"

She shakes her head. "I won't leave you. I promise. Just trust me."

"I trust you, mama." And I do, I trust her more than anyone else, she's all I've got in the whole entire world.

She starts pulling the pill bottles out of my hands. "I'm sorry I scared you. Let me just go put these back in the medicine cabinet."

Reluctantly, I let go, but only after she gave me another

long hug, and whispered in my ear, "You're becoming such a good man, Logan. I'm so proud of you."

I hugged her back, hard. Maybe we'd make it after all…

Except that the next morning I found her dead in her bathtub, bottles of empty pills strewn on the ground.

THIRTY

Present Day
Daphne

When I finally make it back to my apartment yet again, still hauling my stupid suitcases around with me, I'm exhausted. Emotionally. Physically. The world is tilted upside down and all I want is to crash for about a hundred years.

Except that there's Logan, pacing back and forth in front of my building like a stalking predator. His hair is wild and he's not even wearing his mask. People are crossing to the other side of the street just to stay away from him.

But all I can think is *Beautiful man. Beautiful beast.*

I needed him and here he is.

I wave at him as soon as I get out of my taxi. "Logan, help me with my stuff."

His face darkens as soon as he sees me. But I hold up a hand. "Don't even start with me. You don't know the day

I've had. At least come into my place so we can talk things out."

I can't imagine a shouting match on a street corner in front of my townhouse.

Please just let him be reasonable and hear me out for once, I pray as we ascend the steps to my apartment. That's all I need from him. I'm making so many sacrifices here and I need to see that he can do the same. That he can sacrifice his pride and listen.

He grabs the bags from me roughly and follows, a hulking, furious black cloud huffing behind me as we go up the stairs. He's silent as I pull out my keys and push open the door to my empty apartment.

If he's surprised by it's emptied out state, he doesn't say a word. Then again, not saying anything is becoming a theme with him. Though, maybe that's a good thing. If I can say my piece, and if he'll actually *listen*—

But as the door slams shut behind him, he barks, "On your knees. Beg for my forgiveness."

I immediately start shaking my head. "Logan, I didn't do what they said. Those pictures aren't—"

"On your knees!" he roars. "Your Master has given you an order!"

Which just pisses me off. I love what he does to my body. I love the way he commands my pleasure and all that I've discovered in that space. But that's not what this is. He's pissed. He thinks I betrayed him. Again. And he won't fucking *listen*.

I peel off my shirt. When he sees the bra I'm wearing— the same one from the pictures—his eyes go as dark as the clouds in the blackest storm.

"Did you enjoy being his whore?"

I fly at him but he catches my wrist before I can slap

him. "I hate you," I hiss in his face. "Nobody hurts me the way you do."

"And you fucking love it," he growls, face still furious as he drags me towards him, slapping my ass hard as soon as he can get his hands on me.

I'm instantly wet. He's right. I'm addicted to him.

He grabs my face and kisses me hard. It's a dominating, devouring kiss. Staking his claim as he slides a huge hand into my panties and pinches my clit within an inch of its life.

I squeal and twist beneath him, but when he releases his hold, the flood of pleasure that hits me like a wave has me buckling under him so that it's only him who's holding me up.

Not for long, though, because soon he's dragging me to the ground, bunching his sweater underneath my head, and shoving my jeans all the way off.

"Please," I can't help begging. "I need you inside me." Maybe if we can connect in this way, then we can start—

"I thought you hated me," he sneers.

I twist underneath him to face him even as I kick off my pants the rest of the way. I search his eyes, so tumultuous with emotion, and I grab the sides of his face, the ruined and the whole, with my hands.

"Logan, we could have everything, if you would just trust me. Listen to me about what happened. And trust me when I say I didn't betray you. That I would never betray you. *Trust me.*"

But it's like my plea is a bucket of ice water on his head. He wrenches away from me. "I can't. You're a liar. You're all liars."

I scramble up to a sitting position. *All?* "Who?"

He looks briefly my way before shaking his head. "Women."

What the hell? But then he's grabbing his shirt off the ground and shrugging it on over his head. "I should never have come here. This was a mistake."

My heart sinks with every step he takes away. He doesn't even look back once as he leaves, the door closing behind him with a resounding *thud*.

THIRTY-ONE

Present Day
Logan

It was my mom all over again. I slam out of the building and people back away in fear. Fine with me. They don't want me? I don't want them either. I hop in my truck and burn rubber as I pull out of the parking lot.

Trust me. Trust me, she said. When the evidence she was lying was sitting right fucking there.

Obviously Mom was going to kill herself that night, no matter what the fuck I said, or what she promised.

And the pictures of Daphne and Archer in the papers—it was the truth in black and white. Words don't mean shit.

There's the truth. And the truth is that no one ever picks me. My mom picked being *dead* over being with me, so big fucking shock that Daph picked Archer with his money and his fucking perfect face and—

I let out a roar in the cab of the truck as I drive back to

the castle. I want to destroy something. I want to rip the whole fucking world apart.

I close my eyes as rage burns in my brain, making me feel like I'm going to self-combust.

Daphne

I SIT on the wood floor of my empty townhouse. My nipples ache. I took out the piercings...because why bother? I'm not Logan's anymore.

I'm not anyone's.

Sacrifice was supposed to bring reward. Why couldn't he trust me? I... I *love* him. Why isn't that enough? I love him so much, it's ripping my heart out.

Maybe it was better back when I was asleep. Back when I didn't know what it felt like to live life in color. When the world was black-and-white and I woke up and went through the motions each day and then went to sleep again and year passed upon year until I eventually moldered away and went back to the earth to become fertilizer for my beloved roses. Circle of fucking life, right? Why did I think I got to be special, but no, I've got to be one of the rare few with an epic love of a lifetime. That's just a fairytale.

My cell phone rings and I answer it on autopilot. I plugged it in as soon as I got here.

"Daphne?" Rachel's voice is half panic, half hopeful.

I hang up and stare at my phone like it's something vile. WTF is she thinking, calling me? After what she did?

My phone buzzes. She's sent me a text.

Rachel: Daphne, I'm sorry. I can explain.

There's little dots that tell me she's still typing, but I furiously type faster.

Me: You have a lot of nerve, texting me rn.

The ellipses disappear.

Me: Adam told me what you did.

And now I just feel tired.

Me: Why? What did I do to you? I thought we were friends?

Rachel: ...

Me: Don't bother explaining. I'm blocking this number.

Rachel: Wait! It's about your dad—

I snatch up the phone and redial her. My face is wet.

"What about my dad?" I ask before she can greet me. I want no niceties from her. I steel myself for more lies.

"Oh, thank gods. Daphne, he's really, really sick."

"What?" The last time I talked to him... was a while ago. He sounded weak but I thought everything was fine.

"You have to go. Now. The truth is, he's in hospice care."

"Hospice?" I cry, scrambling to my feet. "But that's... That's end-of-life care. Are you just trying to fuck with me again? Why are *you* calling, telling me this and not his nurse?" *After all that you've done!*

"I'm not proud of the way things turned out. Look, I can explain," her voice drops to a whisper. "Just...not now. There's no time. Go, Daphne. If you go now, you might make it in time."

My heart jumps to my throat.

I'm already out the door, flying down the stairs. "Taxi!" I shout. A yellow Chariot wrenches out of traffic to glide to the curb.

"Make it in time for what?" I ask Rachel, but she's quiet

as I tumble into the cab's backseat and give directions to the driver. When I look down at my phone, she's hung up, but a new text has come through.

Rachel: IN TIME TO SAY GOODBYE.

Ten minutes later, I'm in a show down with the stone-faced nurse blocking the entrance to my dad's room.

"He's sleeping," she whispers harshly.

"It's the middle of the day. How long has he been out?"

The nurse's gaze flits away. I clench my fist so I don't grab the front of her shirt and shake her until she tells me what the hell is going on.

Instead, I steel my voice. "How long?"

"This is against protocol," the nurse says to the wall. She's scared of something and I don't understand. "Your father is very ill."

"How ill?" I force myself to sound calm. "Another stroke?"

The nurse finally meets my gaze a second before dropping hers and nibbling on her lip. "Yes. Followed by acute encephalopathy."

The scientist part of my brain scrambles to translate. My voice hitches as I ask, "How bad is it?"

"We started hospice procedures two days ago."

"What?" I whisper-shout. Rachel was right. The realization blasts the hairs on my arm, makes them rise. "Why didn't you tell me it was this bad?"

"We had our orders."

"What orders? From *who*?" my voice jumps an octave and I take a breath trying to calm myself down. "I hired you. I'm his daughter."

The nurse gives a little whimper, and I realize I've backed her into the wall. "Your fiancé," she says desperately. "He told us you had a breakdown and were hospitalized—"

"What?" I screech. No wonder she's looking at me like I'm an escapee from the asylum.

"We were supposed to allow you to talk to your dad but all serious communication should go to Mr. Archer."

Adam fucking Archer. Again. Something's rotten in New Olympus and all roads lead to my bleached blond tabloid co-star. But I don't have time to figure this out. Hospice care means I don't have much time left with my dad.

"I'm going in. You can't stop me from seeing my father." Not if he's on his deathbed. Holy shit, how is this happening? This can't be happening.

"I have to phone this in," the nurse mumbles.

I grab her arm and she flinches. *She thinks I'm crazy.* With a deep breath, I relax my grip. "Please. I'm not asking you to break protocol, just...wait as long as you can. This is my last chance..." *To say goodbye.*

The nurse presses her lips together, summons her humanity, and nods. I duck past her and tiptoe into my dad's room.

Inside it's dark and it smells like sickness. I've been around hospitals enough to recognize that sour scent not even antiseptic can cut. My dad is a shrunken shell of a man. Small and frail sleeping in his bed. I creep to his side and take a seat. The only sound is the soft wheeze of my dad's breathing.

It wasn't supposed to end like this. He was supposed to be getting better. Adam kept this a secret—but why?

You always sensed he was untrustworthy. I thought my instincts were broken. Turns out they were right all along.

If Rachel hadn't called me, I would've missed this. Which means...I don't know what it means.

"I don't know what's real anymore," I whisper. My

dad's eyes remain closed, his mouth slightly open. A sound creaks in his throat, but it's probably involuntary. He's probably just asleep. His index finger twitches on the coverlet.

I bow my head and take hold of his hand. It's all I can do.

THIRTY-TWO

20 years ago
Daphne

"Daphne!" My mother's voice finds me in my hiding place. "Come out from there."

I hold my breath and hug the ground in case she doesn't know I'm actually in the garden.

"I see you behind the forsythia. Come, sweetheart, come help me dig."

I crawl out from under the hedge and run to my mother. She sees the mud and grass stains on my knees, but doesn't scold. She's in an old pair of jeans with matching stain, and her beautiful hands are covered in black dirt.

"What are we planting?" I ask after my own hands are coated in loam.

"Roses."

"More roses?" Every other plant in this garden is a type

of rose. Clipped into hedges, climbing up trellises, or blossoming in pots Mom can move in and out of our house.

Mom laughs. "Always."

"Now we plant." Mom takes a wet paper bag full of green sticks and starts setting them in the earth.

I wrinkle my nose and pick at a shriveled brown leaf. "They look dead."

"They're not dead. They're dormant. Waiting to be planted."

My dad walks by the open window, the phone pressed to his ear. I can't hear what he's saying, but even if I could, I wouldn't understand it. He stands looking out at the garden, but he doesn't seem to really see it. Doesn't see us.

Mom and I plant another five sticks before he hangs up. For a few blissful moments, the only sound is a low buzzing of bees moving from blossom to blossom.

"Piers, come plant with us," my mom waves. My dad holds up a finger, and goes back to typing in another number to call.

I sit back on my haunches. "He's always talking to someone."

"He works hard. That's his job, to take care of us."

Dad starts talking again, leaving a message. The sound of his voice triggers a memory I feel deep in my bones. I grab my aching arms. "Am I going to have to go back to the hospital?"

Mom sees me shrinking into myself, and gives me a hug that leaves dirt prints on my shirt. She smells so sweet, like roses. "No, sweetie. No more hospitals. At least, not for a while."

"How are my two girls?" Dad's shadow falls over me. My mother turns and the sun falls full on her face. Green eyes, black hair and brows, brown skin - she's so beautiful, my mother. My skin is more olive, a compromise between the natural tan of my mother's heritage and my dad's pallor, but otherwise people say I look like her.

"We're planting roses."

"More roses?" Dad teases. And I smile, because that's exactly what I said. But in the next moment he frowns. "Daphne, you're watching out for your momma, right? Make sure she's not growing too tired—"

"That's not her job," Mom's voice is soft, but she rarely cuts people off. Dad stills like she snapped at him.

I pat his leg. "It's okay, Dad. I am watching her. I don't want to go back to the hospital."

Mom and Dad share a long look over my head. It ends when Dad bows his. I don't quite know what their fight is about, but I know Mom won.

"Good girl," Dad says to me. His voice is thick with emotion I don't understand. He drops a kiss on my head and lowers himself down to the lawn with us. "Now, how do I plant these sticks?"

THIRTY-THREE

Present day
Daphne

I don't know how long I sit beside my sleeping father.

He looks bad. Shocking. When did his skin become so translucent? How did I miss this? It's only been a few weeks. He was so much stronger the last time I was here. Now, he looks like he's— Like he's—

I want to reach out and grab his hand but he looks too weak to touch. Like he's made of dust and if I touch him he'll disintegrate.

The nurse comes in and out a few times. Checks my dad's vitals and shows me how to swab his lips to keep them wet. Her stance has softened towards me. Who knows what lies Adam told her about me? Which makes me wonder: what other lies has he told? There is a common denominator in a lot of the bad things that have happened: Adam Archer. But I can't think about that right now.

"Daphne?" my dad's wan voice comes out as the barest whisper through cracked lips. His eyes are open only the barest of slits.

"Dad," I lean in to touch his cheek. *Don't cry. Don't cry.* It feels dry and delicate like filo pastry dough. "I'm here, Dad. It's going to be okay."

"You look...like your mother. I thought you were her."

Crap, now I'm crying. "I was thinking of her just now." I brush my sleeve over my eyes and grab the cup of water. "Hey, can you drink a little bit for me?"

Everything else feels so silly and unimportant now. All the drama. All the hurt and grudges. In this moment, all I want is to go back and spend time with my dad. I wasted so much time. We both did.

"Try..." he whispers. I set the straw between his lips and coax him to take some sips. He doesn't take much. That's when I know: we're counting the hours, not the days, now. Shit.

Fat tears roll down my cheeks. "I didn't know you were this bad. I would've been here. *Dad.*"

"Busy...girl." His eyes are open a little wider now and they are shining, a small smile curving his lips up.

"Yeah." My laugh is pathetic. "It certainly has been a couple of days." I filter through all that's happened, trying to figure out what I can tell him. *Hey, dad, I ended up in the tabloids again—this time with my clothes off! And I've lost the love of my life and my job all in one scandal. Oh, and I think Adam Archer orchestrated it all so he can steal our company.*

"Um, Dad? I have to tell you... I'm not engaged." I stare at his liver-spotted finger entwined with mine. "I told Adam I didn't want to marry him." There, that's nice and simple, and without any lurid details. And I managed not to call Adam a douche canoe.

Dad makes a little sound and I rush out, "I know it's what you wanted for me—"

He seems agitated and finally manages to bark out, "No."

"No?" I risk raising my eyes to his. Is this what it's finally come to, then? And he doesn't even know the worst of it. How do I tell him his life's work, his company is about to slip through my fingers? "I'm such a failure." It's barely a whisper but he must hear.

"Shhh. Not a failure. Never." His hand traces my wrist, the veins, as if remembering when they bore IVs.

"I couldn't save mom. I was supposed to cure her. That's why you had me, right?" I half laugh. But we're both crying.

"Daphne," he mouths my name. Twin tracks of water stream from his eyes.

"Shhh." I wipe his face and give him more water. The nurse comes in and the moment is broken. I excuse myself to give dad privacy.

I find a bathroom and commandeer a whole box of tissues. Then the floodgates open. When I head back in, Dad's sleeping, so I take up vigil by the window and look at the flowers perched in the window box, bright and colorful in the midday sun.

I wasted so much time working for my father's love. Why? *Because you didn't know love could be effortless. Unconditional.* Not like I do now.

The nurse finds me still staring out the window.

"He's ready for you."

I sniffle and wipe my eyes, to hide my sadness. "This is

the end, isn't it?" I can't believe I'm really asking that question.

She hesitates, and nods. "He's out of pain. I did my best to make him comfortable."

"Thank you." I swallow hard.

"Is there anything I can get you?"

"No." I wave the pathetic crumple of tissues in my hand. "I'm fine." The nurse doesn't move, so I add, "I'll go in in a moment."

"I called him. Mr. Archer. I didn't tell him you were here."

"Oh....thank you." I don't quite understand her determined expression, but she looks like she wants to say more.

She draws herself up. "I told him Dr. Laurel wasn't long for this world, and it was time to notify his next of kin. He told me he'd handle it, and hung up."

Ah. Good ole Adam, showing his true douche canoe colors. "He's probably not going to call me."

"That's what I suspected. I saw the tabloids today."

Oh no. "You did?' I hide my wince.

"I did. And if any man did that to me, I wouldn't be his fiancée for long."

I blink at her declaration. "Did...what exactly?" I ask carefully.

"Forced you to have a threesome." She looks as confused as I feel. "At least that's what the Herald said."

"Oh..." A threesome? Dear gods. These reporters have quite the imagination. "Well, you're right. I'm not his fiancée any more. Gave back the ring and everything."

She gives a satisfied nod. "Good girl."

"I told my father the engagement's off, but didn't tell him why."

She mimes locking her lips shut and bustles off.

I wilt against the window. Since when is my life a soap opera? I head back in to my dad, squeezing the back of my neck to wring out the exhaustion.

My dad is sleeping again, his lips parted.

The death rattle starts at dusk. I alternate pacing the floor at the foot of dad's bed, and sitting by his side, watching the blanket rise and fall. Waiting for the final breath.

My dad's lips move and his eyes flutter open. "I wish…"

I rush to grab his cup of ice chips, but he refuses. He's trying to tell me something.

I lean closer. "What, Dad? What do you wish?"

"I wish … Logan were here."

Oh. My. Gods.

I glance at my phone, but it's dead. And Logan probably wouldn't even pick up if I called.

"I had two sons, one dark, one light. Both were lost. But you…" His head rolls back, his eyes fluttering closed as his throat works soundlessly.

His lips move, his voice creaking, "Want you to…" he heaves for breath and continues, "be happy."

My eyes burn. "Oh, Dad."

Finally, after years—after a *lifetime*—of not communicating, I feel like Dad is finally telling me something true. He's finally looking at me and seeing *me*. Talking to me like I'm a real person and not just his creation he can order around.

I see what I couldn't for so long—my father is far from a perfect man. But it doesn't mean there isn't still love between us.

I hold the straw to his mouth again. He takes half a sip of water and chokes out. "You're so beautiful. My rose bud."

"No more time. Need you to—" he heaves and coughs, "forgive me."

"What are you talking about, Dad?"

"It's not right…what we did to him."

Chills blast down my arms. "Dad? What did you do?"

"It's not right," he murmurs weakly. "Adam said…" He shakes his head and his voice trails off. I fight a scream. All my answers are here.

He clutches my hand. "Make it right."

"How?" I cry, but his head has dropped back on the pillow and he starts whispering too softly for me to hear. I put my ear by his lips.

"Bella…"

"Belladonna?" I step back and search my dad's face, but his eyes are closed. He never reopens them, but even unconscious, he continues to whisper one name over and over.

And it's not his company's. It's my mother's.

"Isabella…Isabella… Bella… Bella, Bella, *Bella*…"

THIRTY-FOUR

Present Day
Logan

Dr. Laurel's memorial service is held near Belladonna's headquarters, in a garden dedicated to patients of Battleman's.

"He fought tirelessly to save them from the ravages of a cruel disease. A disease that claimed his wife's life," intones the priestess.

I lurk on the furthest edge of the crowd at the back, watching Daphne's dark, huddled figure. She stands alone beside a display of roses, her face lifted to the misting rain. She looks so cold.

The board members are all here, and so is Adam Archer. The question is, why am *I* here? Just to torment myself?

Did I think I'd feel some sense of victory, standing on

the grave of one of the men who participated in my downfall?

I feel nothing for the old man. But my eyes are continually drawn back to Daphne, again and again. She lived her life for her father's approval for so long. How is she doing now that he's gone?

When the priestess is done with the last rites, my blood burns as Adam makes his way close to Daphne, leaning down to say something to her, but she stares past him to her father's closed coffin. After a few minutes, Adam gives up and stalks away, and my tense muscles relax.

The ceremony continues. Both Adam and the board unerringly find the biggest philanthropists in the city to stand next to, probably so they can schmooze them after the service.

Daphne stays where she is, beside her father's empty coffin. I know it's empty, because earlier today he was cremated. His estate lawyer sent me notice, along with a formal request to be interred beside his wife at Thornhill.

A request I denied. Maybe it's petty of me, but I hated that old bastard and I swore he'd never enter my property dead or alive. He did nothing for his wife or daughter in life.

I feel a few pangs of guilt as Daphne sprinkles rose petals at the base of the statue dedicated to Dr. Laurel. She looks thinner and paler than I last saw her. Reporters dog her steps and I want to growl, scare them all off. Wrap her in my great coat and carry her back to my castle. Make sure she got a good meal in her.

And then what? She chose Adam. I trusted her with my heart and she reduced it to rubble. Why the *fuck* am I here again?

A funeral goer glances up at me, startled. I'm growling

like a feral dog. I glare at him until he flashes the whites of his eyes and scuttles away.

Calm. Control. Daphne's pale face, red lips moving as she thanks the priestess. Her frozen expression as black-garbed people mill past to pay their respects.

I feel nothing for her. I squeeze my hands into fists and tell myself that over and over again. I can believe anything if I say it enough times. Any emotion I ever had for Daphne Laurel needs to die.

Daphne

LOGAN LEAVES. A hulking mountain of a man. I saw him as soon as he showed up. It's ridiculous that he even tries to hide.

Adam Archer leaves too, after posing with the statue for a few photos. He glances my way, willing me to look at him, but the board gathers around him, ushering him away. Belladonna's board members won't even look in my direction.

Not that I want them to. The news came out this morning: Belladonna's CEO fired. The papers took the opportunity to rerun my half-naked photos on the front page. Next to the news of my dad's memorial service.

I lost everything in one fell swoop.

Half the people came to pay their respects, the other half to gawk. Or take photos of me, the disgraced daughter. Not that I need more photographic evidence to document my complete and utter failure.

"I'm sorry for your loss," a well meaning socialite murmurs.

Which one? I want to reply.

"I'd say I'm sorry for your loss, but I'm more worried about you catching cold," a cultured voice makes my chin jerk up.

Armand. Seeing a friendly face in this tank of sharks is so welcoming, I have to fight back tears as Armand grasps both my hands in his gloved ones.

"Girl, you need more layers." He starts stripping off his gloves.

"What are you doing?" I ask, but I let him take my hand and tug the glove on.

He doesn't answer until he's put both of his gloves on my hands. I haven't cried since my dad died, but Armand's kindness makes me want to weep. "I heard about what happened. With Belladonna, with everything. I know it's trite, but I believe things will turn out all right." He touches my face and now his hands are cold. "How're you doing?"

I tell him the honest truth. "I'm at rock bottom." There's no one left, nowhere to go. I'm all but homeless, friendless, have no more family, no job, no—

"Come here." Armand hugs me in front of everyone. Not that there are many people left and I don't care who's watching anyway. It's not like I have much reputation left to lose.

"You know the great thing about rock bottom?" Armand's whisper tickles my ear. "There's nowhere to go but up."

I choke out a laugh and pull away from Armand. "Thank you," I sniffle.

"And look on the bright side. You look wicked lovely in black." His kohl-lined eyes glitter with laughter, and I reward him with a small smile. "Next time—a hat. A hat would complete this look. Funeral chic."

"I'll keep it in mind." I bite back my own smile. And gods, he's right. I'm not the one who died today. If I'm lucky, I'll have a long, full life. I can't just give up because of a rough patch. Even if it's a *really* rough patch.

The last of the crowd flocks away, leaving me beside the statue honoring my dad. A pigeon has already crapped on the bronze head. But that's life, isn't it?

"Bye, Dad."

My bones creak as I head to the curb. I feel old, like I've aged ninety years in a week. But my heart is light. Maybe Armand is right. Rock bottom is a great place to be.

At my feet, a little yellow blossom pokes up between two slabs of concrete. A dandelion growing through the cracks. Most people would call it a weed, but my mother knew ten different ways to use the blossom, leaves, and root.

I can do this.

I luck out and catch up to Armand before he gets in the car.

"Daphne? You need a ride?"

"No," I blurt, then amend. "Well, actually yes. That'd be great. But really I need a favor. Something delivered."

A smile spreads across his face. "Well, then, I'm your messenger."

THIRTY-FIVE

Present Day
Logan

I pace the sidewalk outside Daphne's apartment. I made it all of about six hours after leaving her at the funeral before hopping in the truck and driving like a bat out of hell back over here.

I might've hated her father but she loved him.

And I remember how broken she was when she lost her mother. How lost she was and how she clung to me like I was the only thing that made sense in her shattered world.

Things were so simple back then. I punched the buzzer again but she doesn't respond. Is she not home or just not responding to me?

The sun is dropping below the horizon and with it, the temperature, but the cold doesn't touch me. I'm already numb from days replaying our last fight in my head.

"Nobody hurts me the way you do."

Why do I even think she's here? She's probably run back to Adam. The thought is acrimonious and bitter going down.

But even as I tell myself that, I don't believe it. *"Trust me when I say I didn't betray you. That I* would *never betray you. Trust me. We could have everything, if you would just trust me."*

I shake my head, growling, and a couple of pedestrians startle and scuttle away.

That's right. Run from the madman.

I tried to go back to the castle. Tried to get on with my life. But I just have to make sure she's okay.

The street lights switch on. I turn up the collar of my great coat. When I close my eyes, I see Daphne's small form at the memorial service. I reach out as if I could touch her, as if my thoughts could conjure her. But when I open my eyes, she's not here.

I pace a few more times, kicking pieces of trash into the gutter before I face her door, and the truth.

She's not coming. Tonight I'll be alone.

Better get used to it.

And just like that, the isolation that is my life hits me with full force. Endless days and nights of me rattling around that huge castle, alone and empty. Soon I really will be a mad old monster.

I turn and almost knock over a slender man in a great coat. He clings to me to keep from falling and I set him upright without cussing him out. My good deed for the day.

But once he's standing on his own, he keeps hold of me. "My gods," he feels the muscle in my arms. "No skipping workouts for you. At least, not arm day."

I open my mouth to snarl and he holds up the last thing I'd expect. A rose.

And that's when I recognize him. He's the man I saw Daphne talking to at the most recent Ubeli ball. Armand. I pulled him aside and told him I was her secret admirer. I asked him to give her the message to meet me in the labyrinth along with her mother's favorite rose. It feels like a lifetime ago now even though it couldn't have been more than a month.

But now he's handing me that exact same species of rose. Then he leans in, kohl-lined eyes twinkling.

"I have a message for you."

"A message," I repeat, fighting the urge to step back. What the hell is this guy playing at? What's his game? He keeps holding the rose in my face until I snatch it away. "Is this it?"

"That's half of it." He hands me a roll of paper tied with a red ribbon.

I'm itching to study both the rose and the note, but not with him watching. "Who are you?"

"Me? I'm just a messenger." He nods at the items I'm holding. "She wanted me to give you these."

She? "Who?"

"You know who."

Fucking riddles. I jerk off the ribbon and unroll the paper just enough to read the first part of the fancy script. *Avicennius Grant...*

I jerk my head up. "Is this...?"

"Daphne's Avicennius grant. And I believe that second piece of paper is her college diploma. One of them."

Sure enough, the paper reads *Awarded to*: and follows with Daph's full name. "I don't understand." What the hell is this? How did he get these? Is he trying to threaten—

"Come on, Wulfe. You can do better than that. Daphne

is smart; she deserves someone to match." He taps the papers. "She sent these clues."

Her award and diploma? How are they clues? "Why would she send these?"

"Fine," Armand sighs in disappointment at my failure to play his made-up game. "I'll spell it out for you. This is all she has left. And she's giving them to you. Get it?" He cocks his head to the side, studying me.

When I still don't give him a satisfactory answer, he just shakes his head and waves his hand like he's done with me. "She wants to see you. You better hurry. She shouldn't be alone."

"Where is she?"

"You know where." He gives me a patient smile. "Where did those papers hang?"

I answer automatically, "In her bedroom at..."

The man touches two fingers to his forehead and flicks them at me before striding off.

I whirl on my heel, crushing the papers in my hand. Only to smooth them out carefully once we're in my car.

"Sir? Where are we headed?"

"Thornhill."

THIRTY-SIX

Present Day
Logan

I give directions and ease back in the seat, clutching my rose like a gold ticket. My invitation back into Daphne's world. Back to where we began.

So much has happened, though. It's not like we can just go backwards. Just because her father died, am I just supposed to forget the pictures...the betrayal?

But maybe, for one night, none of that matters.

She shouldn't be alone. What did Armand mean by that? Is she... I shake my head. Daphne isn't like my mom.

But when the driver pulls up to Thornhill, it's dark. No light in the windows. Including the ones I broke.

Shards of glass line my throat when I think of Daphne seeing how I smashed her childhood home.

"Should I wait, sir?" the driver asks.

"No. Come back in the morning." Even if Daphne isn't

here, I'll stay. I'll spend the night in the only place that ever felt like home...and then only for one night. Because I was with her.

The floorboards creak and puffs of dust rise like ghosts. I turn in a circle, remembering when this place was beautiful. I never should've bought it. I ruin everything I touch.

"Daphne," I whisper. The stairs groan under my weight. But then I see it—a flicker of light in the far corner of the house.

In her old room. Of course.

"Hello? Daphne?"

"In here," she calls.

I rush down the rest of the hall and stand dumbfounded in the door. Daphne stands in the light of a single candle. The weak flame casts more shadows than light, emphasizing the dirty smudges on her face and furrows of exhaustion under her eyes.

She looks so beautiful.

"Welcome to my humble abode," she waves a hand around her dark and dank room. She's taken the curtains I ripped down and made a bed in the corner. Next to it is a table with a broken leg, propped up with books, that holds the candle. "It's not much, but it's all I've got, for now."

She's grinning.

"Daphne...are you okay?" *She shouldn't be alone,* Armand had said. With everything that's happened, has she suffered a mental break?

"Never better."

I cross to her, reach out to touch her flushed cheek, but my finger hovers in the air. "You're freezing."

"I'm fine. I was cuddled up with some of these fine curtains before I heard you."

I'm already removing my overcoat. "Let's get you warm."

"No more trials? No more labors of Hercules?" she murmurs as she lets me wrap her in the dark wool. It drapes around her like over-sized wizard robes.

"No. No more games." This time, I do touch her face. Her skin is cold, but not as bad as I thought. "What are you doing here?"

"Here? Well..." she laughs, her head falling back, which makes her hair cascade in a lush black waterfall. She looks so carefree, it's freaking me out. Especially when she continues, "Dad's estate is in probate. My townhouse was actually a perk of working at Belladonna so now that I'm no longer there, I don't have a—"

"Wait...you're not at Belladonna?"

"Nope." Her head tilts to the side as she stares at me. "Where have you been? Didn't you see the news?"

I could hardly miss it. The business newspapers in particular reported her termination as CEO with glee. "I thought they'd just demote you."

"Oh no, they were real thorough about throwing me out." She doesn't seem concerned. She squats and pulls up the over-sized sleeve so she can rustle around in a half empty knapsack lying beside her makeshift bed.

A few seconds later, she holds up a protein bar. "Hercules bar? They're actually pretty good. They have ten times the daily dosage of every vitamin, which is overkill and might possibly make a person sick, but I can't resist the ones dipped in chocolate."

She studies the bodybuilder on the package. "You know, if the reclusive dom gig doesn't work out for you, you could probably model for this company— "

"Daphne! What happened? Why are you—" I look

around at the shambles of her dark room.

"Living like a homeless person in my former home?" She doesn't lose that light-hearted smile. "Well, when did we last speak? Oh yeah, the night you walked out on me because someone drugged me and took photos of me half-nekkid. The night before my dad died."

Her matter-of-fact tone doesn't stop each statement from slamming into me like a bullet. *Drugged her?* What the—

"Our relationship is super fucked up, Logan," she adds, and smacks her lips as she eats the chocolate bar. "But," her voice softens. "I'm glad you're not wearing the mask. I saw you at the funeral without it."

"Enough." I growl before she continues in this ridiculous vein and compliments my neck beard. "Daphne, nothing's changed between us. Tell me why I should trust you."

"Oh, so now you're willing to listen?" she raises a brow.

I swallow. "I was wrong. I should've listened before."

"Yes, you should've," she says, settling cross-legged on the pile of curtains. "From the very start and every time afterwards, you should've listened to me before flying off the handle. I know I didn't handle things well and you had reasons for your questions. Good reasons. But I didn't deserve what you did to me."

"You liked everything I did—

She waves a hand impatiently. "I'm not talking about all that. I did love that. I do. I love everything you've given me. The truth is, Logan, I love you."

She loves me. Bright sunshine bursts inside my chest even as a voice in the back of my mind screams, *can't trust her, can't trust her, can't trust*—

"But part of becoming the woman you've helped me discover, is that I refuse to be treated badly. I've done everything in my power to prove my devotion and loyalty. But it's never enough. You'll always believe outside voices over mine. I was drugged, my privacy violated, and you believed my accusers over me. Do you know what that feels like?"

Just like that, I feel like I've been kicked in the gut. I never even thought about that before and—

"Remember that night in the labyrinth?" she continues relentlessly. "Remember what happened to me?"

I crouch down to get closer to her level, and also because I don't feel so steady on my feet as the pieces come together. "You fainted. You were drugged."

She touches her forehead with a finger and flicks at me. Much like Armand did. Have they been hanging out?

Jealousy snarls through me but I push it aside to process what she's saying. "You were drugged." I can't believe I didn't guess it before now. Maybe I am as slow as Armand insinuated.

"Yep." She pops the 'p'. "You get one guess as to who did it."

"Adam." I straighten in the doorway. My hands come up as if grabbing an imaginary man to rip apart. "I'll kill him." I told myself I was going to that engagement party to protect her but all I did was leave her vulnerable. All I could see was my stupid revenge and he, he—

Daphne rises too and approaches me without fear. "That's not the whole story. After you and I had our little conversation, I got news that my dad was dying. I had no idea his health had gotten so bad. Adam didn't want me to know."

"What?" I feel my face and neck flaming red. Like gasoline poured on my rage.

"It didn't work. I talked to dad before he died." She cups my face in her hands. Her touch calms the Beast. "Logan, he told me he was sorry for how things turned out. For what he and Adam did to you."

"He...did?"

And the blows just keep coming. I barely get my balance before another blow all but knocks me off my feet.

"He did." Her voice is gentle. Kind. "Unfortunately it was too late for me to get more details, so I could get proof or a confession against Adam, but if we dig, I bet we can find it."

We?

My heart leaps. She's talking about the future. Our future. But I failed her, over and over. How can she—?

"So that's everything that happened," she says, "until Tuesday happened."

"What happened Tuesday?" Fuck, I'm not sure how much more I can take.

"That's when I met with the board. They voted me out. But I still gave them copies of this." She spins around to dig in her bag until she comes up with a sheet of paper, neatly folded.

I snatch it and read it with my phone's flashlight. "You...resigned?"

"Yep." Her voice turns more serious. "I have nothing, Logan. Not a thing. Just two dead parents, my degrees, and the Avicennius grant. Except that I sent you those two pieces of paper. So, technically, nothing. I have nothing, Logan." She doesn't look sad or bitter. She looks... calm. At peace. "I'm finally free. Completely free." She flops her arms outwards. "It only took losing everything," she laughs.

It doesn't change the fact that she's squatting in the ruined shell of her childhood home. Like a homeless person. Even in my great coat, she looks cold.

I've been the world's biggest asshole.

This, in front of me, is my Daphne, the same as she ever was. Innocent of the world's malice. Pure in all the ways that matter. She wasn't trying to play rivals against one another or win fame or fortune. She has nothing and yet she still manages to be happy. And after everything I did, she can still look in my monster's face and without batting an eye tell me she loves me.

She's a fucking angel gracing this earth in a sexy-as-sin body.

"Anyway, I just wanted to tell you that. Thank you for coming." She pats the pockets of my coat, pulls out the papers and the rose. "I had a hell of the time convincing Armand to leave me here. He made me swear up and down I'd call him if you didn't show up."

"I'll call him," I say quickly.

"Are you jealous of Armand? Don't be." She lays everything on the table, then pulls on a pair of gloves. They look too large, but at least it's something. She still looks cold, though. I don't like it.

"You can't stay here," I say gruffly.

She raises a brow. "You're kicking me out?"

"Yes... No! I'm not kicking you out. I mean, you should be at the castle, with me."

"You hurt me, Logan." Just a whisper, and it's a dagger through my chest. I stumble back and lean against the door frame so I don't fall to my knees.

"I know." I tear a hand through my hair. My face feels naked without the mask. "I don't trust easy. Or at all."

"You haven't had reason to," she murmurs.

"No, don't do that." I point at her. "Don't make excuses for me. I'm a monster."

"You're my monster." She sways forward slowly, carefully, as if approaching a wild animal.

"I don't know what I can do to earn your forgiveness." I can't believe all this time I was trying to make her prove her love and devotion to me, when I should have been begging at her feet the entire time.

"You don't have to earn my love, Logan. I'm giving it to you."

And I sink to my knees. "Daphne."

She kneels and hugs me, snuggling her head to my chest. Her weight over my heart…it's everything.

"I gave everything up for you," she whispers. "Belladonna. The patents…I'm not with you for them. I've let them all go. I want you *for you*."

"I don't know what I did to deserve this." She's breaking me, doesn't she realize that? No one ever wants me. I'm a shit. I'm worthless. My own mom didn't think I was worth sticking around for. No foster family ever wanted me. Even Dr. Laurel threw me away when I became inconvenient.

There's no way this goddess could actually want the dirty little boy whose mom couldn't even remember to feed him.

But she clutches my face and forces me to look her in the eyes.

"You woke me up. I get to live my life starting now. And I choose you." She shivers, and I stop fighting my protective impulses and wrap her up in my arms. Or maybe I need it as much as she does. I need to hold her and feel that she's real. I still can't believe that happiness like this could actually be in reach for someone like me.

"Stay with me, Logan," she whispers and I hold her tighter. "I don't know who I am, or what I'm going to do, or where I'm going, but I want you. Not because of the patents. Not because of our past. Because of who you are … and who we could be."

THIRTY-SEVEN

Present Day
Daphne

The creaking floor wakes me. I blink in the honeyed morning light.

I haven't slept this well since...since the last time Logan held me until I fell asleep. The bed is warm but he's not beside me.

The lights are on. Huh. I squint and look around. My bedroom's wallpaper is still faded, but the floor is swept clean...and everything smells like lemon cleanser. I sit up and that's when I notice that I'm not lying on a pile of curtains anymore, but a legit mattress hovering off the ground on some sort of frame. And I'm super warm because I'm wrapped in a brand new looking sleeping bag.

"I thought you'd wake when I moved you to the camp bed, but you must have been tired," Logan says from the door. I grin at the deep sound of his voice and look his way.

And damn, he's *fine*. He's dressed in jeans and a flannel shirt instead of the suit from last night. He's holding a bunch of roses. And when I catch his gaze, well, let me tell you, I feel it all the way down to my lady bits.

"Are those for me?" I ask, pulling the sleeping bag up to my chin, feeling ridiculously shy and terribly happy all at the same time.

"Always." He sits carefully on the edge of the bed and hands them to me. I immediately bury my face in the flowers.

"A bit early for these to bloom."

"I had them delivered from my greenhouse. Along with..." he leans down and reaches into a giant hamper of food beside the bed. I gape at the full picnic spread laid out on a big plaid blanket. There's even a mini propane stove with a shiny stovetop espresso maker.

"Oh my gods, Logan. Are we glamping?" I look up at him, excited.

Everything has just been so damn heavy lately. But after last night's reconciliation...I have to say, I adore the playful spark in Logan's eyes. I can't remember the last time I saw it. He seems totally open, finally nothing held back. The boy I once knew in the body of the man I love.

He shrugs and uncaps a bottle of sparkling water. "Just until this place gets cleaned up. I turned the electricity back on. The water, too." He takes the roses back and trades me the water bottle.

"I wanted you to wake up surrounded by roses. The garden's overgrown, but I've made arrangements for gardeners and contractors to come. They'll fix this place. I'll fix everything."

I lay my hand on his stubble roughed jaw. He turns his face and kisses my palm.

"You want to live here?" My laugh bounces between the bare walls. Only they're not so bare, because he's found the old frame for my diploma and awards, and rehung them.

"If you want. Daphne, I'll give you everything. Just...come back to me."

LOGAN

SHE'S LOOKING at me with the whole world in her eyes. "Daphne?" I can't bring myself to repeat my plea. I can only hope she'll say yes.

"Silly man," she says, "I never left."

My exhale is half groan. I don't move, afraid to break this moment. Afraid it will shatter. I'll wake up from this dream.

"Daphne." Her name is a light and I'm a lost man, staggering towards salvation.

"Logan. I choose you. I love *you*."

Her words send electricity shooting through my body. I'll never get tired of her saying that. In fact I think I'll make her say it about a thousand times every day, and maybe two thousand times a day on the weekends. This sleeping bag is brand new, but it's in the way. I rip it open to free her. I need to be inside her...now.

Daphne lets off peals of laughter, like little bells. Gods, she's adorable. "What's the rush? We have time."

"Need you," I grunt, dragging off my jeans. She has no idea. The fact that I managed to leave her alone last night was a miracle.

Daphne stretches out on the mattress. I ease her panties

off and lean in to kiss her flat stomach. My dick is so hard it might split, but I catch a whiff of her perfume, and I can't resist climbing down her body and burying my face in her muff.

"Logan, ah, Logan," she chants. Her hands bat at my shoulders and I capture them, pinning them down. One more taste. Just one more. And another. I swipe my tongue over her fragrant pussy, long, lingering drags to savor all her sweetness. Doesn't she understand? I need to devour her. I need to convince myself she's real. She's mine and she's real and she's here and this is actually happening and this can be forever—

Her body bows off the bed as far as I'll let it. Her cries of pleasure crash around me and still I delve my tongue into her folds, chasing her essence. Fuck, I love her taste and watching her absolutely lose it.

"Give it to me," I order when she protests it's too much. "Now, Daphne. I want it all."

Her slender legs shake and drum on my back as my tongue sends her body higher and higher. When she finally lies limp, I rise up and climb gingerly onto the camp bed. I rush ordered the frame and mattress so Daphne wouldn't spend another night on the floor, but it's way too spindly for my weight.

I'm shaking as I guide myself in between her legs. No bells or whistles this time. I just need my body connected to hers. I need the intimacy and to just bury myself in her. So deep, I want to disappear inside her. And Daphne is just as eager, urging me on with breathy pleas and little kisses that make me grit my teeth so I don't blow too soon.

As I rock into position, the camp bed crashes to the floor. Shit!

"Logan!" Daphne is laughing so hard, tears stream from her eyes.

"Fucking piece of crap," I mutter, arms around her body to protect her from the wreckage.

"We killed it," Daphne cackles, curling into my arms and lifting her hands to clutch around my neck.

"I was trying to be gentle." I lift her off the ruined bed and kick the mattress away from the frame so I can lay her back down.

Her laughter subsides, leaving a soft expression that makes me ache. "I don't want gentle." Her fingers trace my stubbled jaw, feeling for the scars underneath. She smiles when she finds them, as if they're a secret we share between us. "I want you. I'm strong, Logan."

"I know you are." I sip at her perfect lips. Gods, this woman is so perfect. So beautiful. So fuckin' smart.

I cup her smooth buttocks and draw her close. "Tell me you want this. Tell me you're mine."

"Always," she begs. "Always."

I ease into her. She's so small and tight, and I'm too big. Moans hum in her chest, but her lithe calf twined around my back tugs me closer. I cup her face and nibble on her lips, rewarding her as she stretches around me slowly. Finally, finally I'm seated inside her.

"Give it to me, Logan," she whispers. "I want it all."

Oh, I'll give it to her. But on my timeline, my way. The woman's already made me lose my head. Besides, this coming back together means something to me and I want her to know that.

So I pin her in place with my cock, exactly where I like her, and I give her my truth. "I love you. I've loved you since you were eighteen and we spent all those summer days at the beach talking—"

She squeezes around me. "You mean you spent all those hours ogling me in my red bikini."

"Vixen."

I grin and grab her wrists, pinning them over her head. I notch my thigh between her legs, bearing down against her sensitive spot until she groans my name.

"That damn red bikini." I shake my head. "I still haven't punished you for teasing me like that all that summer, have I?"

She stretches up and nips me on the jaw with her teeth. Somebody's feeling playful.

But then she pulls back and goes serious again. "I can't believe my dream finally came true," she whispers. "I can't believe Logan Wulfe actually loves me back."

How am I supposed to have any control after she says something like that? I don't bother even trying. I thrust inside her, giving us what we are both craving, and we moan in tandem.

Pleasure flashes up my sides, unknots my spine, nearly blinds me. There's no holding back after that. I saw in and out of her perfect, tight entrance, making sure to grind against her clit with each pass.

"Harder." Her nails dig into my shoulders. "Harder!"

She's the perfect woman made flesh. I ram her so hard the mattress hits the wall. The frames above us shudder, but the screws I used hold.

She starts to shatter around me.

"I'm gonna give you everything, Daphne. Every hope. Every dream." I roll my hips, prolonging each thrust, and tears stream from her eyes. Tears of joy.

Her body stiffens, her pussy massaging my cock as she cums over and over. And as I cum, I make a vow.

To be hers. To be Daphne's. She knows all my evil

desires, how I lust to hurt the ones I love. My past, my present, my wickedness. She's walked every twisting turn of the labyrinth and come out the other side.

And still she loves me. She chose me.

My vision blurs and I blink my eyes to clear them. The view isn't great—four dirty walls of this dilapidated room but I'm seeing them fresh.

With Daphne, I can have it all. A life. A full heart. A family.

For the second time in my life, I've come home.

THIRTY-EIGHT

Present Day
Daphne

"So what about Adam?" I ask. I hate to break the mood, but I can't take any more sex. Not after Mr. Insatiable ate me a second time, and flipped me over to pound me from behind. This poor mattress is done for.

"What about him?" Logan's voice is level, but his body hardens to a block of stone. I massage his neck, but it's like trying to get granite to relax.

I rise up and lean into his back, blowing into his ear. His shoulders ease a fraction.

"I think he should pay for what he's done," I murmur into one ear, and switch to the other. Just like being with Logan has taught me not to deny any of who I am, I don't want to deny any of who Logan is. At the same time... "But I don't want you to end up in jail for homicide."

"It won't be homicide. I want him to suffer."

"I thought I was the only one you tortured." I pretend to pout. Let's keep this light. "Are you telling me this isn't exclusive?"

"What I do to you isn't torture," he says as I nibble on his ear. "You like it too much."

"Maybe I should torture you..."

With a sudden move, he twists and pulls me onto his lap. "Little seductress. Trying to change my mind with your wiles?"

"It it working?" I wriggle in his lap. "Feels like it." His boner is the size of a tree. There's so much good here. I don't want to let Adam or anyone else to ruin it.

He lets me grind on his lap for about a second longer, then maneuvers me until I'm flat on my back with his big body caging me. My pussy is sopping, my breath coming in pants, ready for his claiming, but he stills.

"Daphne, I can't change who I am." He says, echoing my thoughts. His eyes search mine, pleading.

I know what he's saying. He can't give up his revenge. He won't. *Not even for me?* asks little voice in my head. But that's not fair. I'm not in his shoes and I can't fathom going through what he went through at Adam's hands.

So I give a tiny nod. As long as we're together and none of his actions involve him being taken from me? I'm on his side, always. He sighs and hugs me, holding his body off me so I'm not crushed. I kiss his neck. Maybe he's not ready to forgive and forget, like I am, but baby steps.

Holding each other like this inevitably leads us back to the—now broken, but when has that ever stopped anyone—bed. His touch drives me insane. I can't get enough.

When we're done making love for the third time, he tests the faucet for hot water. With a steaming face cloth he wipes down my body carefully. He pays special attention to my breasts.

"You took the piercings out." He sounds sad.

"I didn't think I could prevent infection in my homeless state. You can re-pierce them."

"No." He drops the washcloth. "I don't want to hurt you anymore."

"You won't. I'll take the thorns with the roses, remember?"

He leans in to kiss me. When our lips part, he presents me with a perfect red rose. "Your rose with thorns."

I grasp the stem. My cheeks are sore from smiling so hard. This love story isn't perfect, but it's ours. And that sorta makes it perfect.

I bring the bloom to my face and inhale. "There. That scent. My mother's perfume, my past and future all rolled into one. It's beautiful."

"It is," Logan says, but he's looking at me. My heart swells.

"I love you, Logan Wulfe."

He smiles, that rakish carefree grin that I love so much. "I love you, t—" he starts to say but then his expression suddenly changes. "Daphne," he rasps, fear etched into the lines on his brow, around his eyes. He reaches out to touch my face, but I beat him to it.

Something wet is trickling from my nose.

I frown. What on ear— My fingers are red when they come away. Blood drips on my palm. Oh shit. The bottom drops out and suddenly I'm sinking, sinking—

Logan rips his white dress shirt and hands me a makeshift handkerchief to press to my nose. His big hand covers my forehead.

"No fever. Just a nosebleed?" His eyebrows pinch together but he doesn't look too concerned.

"It's not just a nosebleed," I close my eyes, wishing I could stop time. No, no no no.

It's not fair. Not when I just found him. Not when we just found *this,* here together.

"Then what? Daphne, what's happening? My gods, I need to call an ambulance." He starts to rise and I catch his arm. I'm weak, so much weaker than him, but he stills at my butterfly light touch.

"No, Logan. No ambulance. Just...stay with me. One minute longer." I throw my arms around him, wishing I could go back to that perfect moment, that single second when I had it all before the gods stripped it all away.

"Daphne, please," Logan eases me back. "Talk to me. What's going on? Are you sick?"

"I'm sick, Logan. I've always been sick. The disease is in my blood."

Horrified awareness dawns on his face as I swallow and pronounce my death sentence.

"I have Battleman's. And it's back."

READ the conclusion to Logan and Daphne's saga, available this spring.

Pre-order Beauty and the Rose now so you don't miss a thing!

Hungry for more dark romance from Lee and Stasia now?

Find out what happens when Marcus, the king of the criminal underworld who always gets what he wants decides to capture the beautiful, innocent Cora, in his web. He'll give her all that her heart desires. Except for one thing. Her freedom. She's his to keep, and he's never letting her go.

One-click Innocence now!

And for a limited time, get these two exclusive books not available anywhere else ABSOLUTELY FREE when you subscribe to Stasia Black's and Lee Savino's newsletter, ***Daddy's Sweet Girl by Stasia Black*** and ***Royally F*cked by Lee Savino.***

ALSO BY STASIA BLACK

DARK CONTEMPORARY ROMANCES

Beauty's Beast

Beauty and the Thorns

Beauty and the Rose

Innocence

Awakening

Queen of the Underworld

Cut So Deep

Break So Soft

Hurt So Good

The Virgin and the Beast: a Beauty and the Beast Tale

Hunter: a Snow White Romance

The Virgin Next Door: a Ménage Romance

SCI-FI ROMANCES

Theirs to Protect

Theirs to Pleasure

Theirs to Wed

Theirs to Defy

Theirs to Ransom

My Alien's Obsession

My Alien's Baby

ALSO BY LEE SAVINO

Lee's books on Amazon

Contemporary romance:

Beauty and the Lumberjacks: a dark reverse harem romance

Her Marine Daddy

Her Dueling Daddies

Royally Fucked - get free at www.leesavino.com

Paranormal & Sci fi romance:

The Alpha Series

The Draekon Series

The Berserker Series

ABOUT STASIA BLACK

STASIA BLACK grew up in Texas, recently spent a freezing five-year stint in Minnesota, and now is happily planted in sunny California, which she will never, ever leave.

She loves writing, reading, listening to podcasts, and has recently taken up biking after a twenty-year sabbatical (and has the bumps and bruises to prove it). She lives with her own personal cheerleader, aka, her handsome husband, and their teenage son. Wow. Typing that makes her feel old. And writing about herself in the third person makes her feel a little like a nutjob, but ahem! Where were we?

Stasia's drawn to romantic stories that don't take the easy way out. She wants to see beneath people's veneer and poke into their dark places, their twisted motives, and their deepest desires. Basically, she wants to create characters that make readers alternately laugh, cry ugly tears, want to toss their kindles across the room, and then declare they have a new FBB (forever book boyfriend).

Join Stasia's Facebook Group for Readers for access to deleted scenes, to chat with me and other fans and also get access to exclusive giveaways:
Stasia's Facebook Reader Group

ABOUT LEE SAVINO

Lee Savino has grandiose goals but most days can't find her wallet or her keys so she just stays at home and writes. While she was studying creative writing at Hollins University, her first manuscript.won the Hollins Fiction Prize.

She lives in the USA with her awesome family. You can find her on Facebook in the **Goddess Group** (which you totally should join).

Printed in Great Britain
by Amazon